Murder at the Expo

Miss Sadie Brown & the Death of Dr. Wolf

P. Austin Heaton

DEDICATION

This novel is dedicated to the amazing people who encouraged and supported me, especially the Wednesday Meditation group and the Writer's Read program

MAIN CHARACTERS

BENNET, **Simon**.....Member of the Francis Drake Research Society & man-about-town.

BROWN, **Sadie**.....Aviatrix and newspaper columnist for the *San Diego News-Herald*.

BROWN, **Equal J**......Famed investigative journalist and Sadie's grandfather.

COHEN, Julius "**Jules**".....Coroner.

GREENWAY, **Evan**.....Sergeant with the SDPD.

HENDERSON, Bartholomew "**Bart**".....Officer with the SDPD.

HELBURG, **Beth**.....Maid for the Wolf family and childhood friend of Lou Wolf.

JAMES, Mr.....Archivist for the *San Diego News-Herald*.

SHINE, Gilbert "**Gil**".....Driver for the Wolf family.

SIEBERT, **Roger**.....Society photographer and boyfriend of Sadie Brown.

SIEBERT, Mrs. **Elizabeth**.....Robert's mother.

TRIGBY, **Rose**.....Nurse at Agnew Sanitarium and Hospital.

WATKINS, Lafayette "**Fayette**".....brother to Lou Wolf and surgeon at Agnew Sanitarium and Hospital.

WOLF, **Asa**.....Murder victim. Head of Surgery and Board Member at Agnew Sanitarium and Hospital.

WOLF, Louise "**Lou**".....Widow of the murder victim.

* * *

FRANCIS DRAKE RESEARCH SOCIETY members: Simon Bennet, Jeffrey Mayfield, Ezra Smith, Asa Wolf.

PHRENOLOGY (pseudoscience study of bumps & structure of the skull to predict mental traits) STUDY CLUB members mentioned by name: Dr. Patrick O'Brien, Dr. Sanders, Dr. Asa Wolf.

CHAPTER 1

July 7, 1915 – Night of the Murder

Angry screams broke the quiet summer night, waking the songbirds in their bamboo cages. With frightened concern, they watched the last of a life and death struggle below. After the shouting and screaming, a heavy, middle-aged man had fallen in a heap unable to move. Over him stood a killer.

With some effort, the over-weight man was positioned just so under a giant fern. Satisfied, the murderer straightened up and spoke. "Don't bother to struggle, Dr. Wolf. It's a type of paralysis is what it is."

Taking a deep breath of gardenia scented night air, the killer sighed. "A bright side...if there is such a thing as a bright side when one is dying...the Botanical Building is a lovely place to breathe your last. And perfect weather, a balmy summer night with a sliver of moon shining through the wood slats."

A blood-stained cloth was folded and pocketed along with a piece of paper. "Too bad you felt the need to throw a punch. I'm going to have to throw away a perfectly good tooth and my favorite handkerchief."

Kneeling, the murderer closed Wolf's eyes using two Buffalo nickels to weigh them shut. "If you're lucky, that bad heart of yours will stop ticking before your lungs shut down. Either way, it'll be quite unpleasant.

"A final thought, Doctor. I'm not a monster. But you push people to the breaking point. This time, you pushed the wrong person. You see that don't you?"

Dr. Asa Wolf said nothing. His vocal cords had stopped working moments before.

The killer turned and left. In their cages, the songbirds ruffled their feathers and drifted back to sleep. Sweet visions of bugs and worms scuttled and squirmed about in their dreams.

CHAPTER 2

July 8, 1915 - Morning after the Murder

The high-pitched scream of a siren could be heard as morning light struggled through Sadie Ann Brown's bedroom window. Pulling back the drapes and rolling up the shade, she peered outside and watched three San Diego Police motorcycles speed past her apartment building. A possible story for some lucky reporter she supposed.

Drying her pixie cut hair, she looked at the note taped to her mirror. It was her father's favorite quote. *It's not the size of the dog in the fight, it's the size of the fight in the dog...Mark Twain.* For some reason, it pleased her to read the quote while she combed her unfashionably cropped hair.

Her father and her famous grandfather, Equal J. Brown, would have been pleased with the haircut and the reason behind the bravura cut. Her loving but conventional mother, probably not. "A sign of girlish rebellion gone too far." Those might have been her exact words.

Patting the pink silk flower on her gray linen suit, securing her straw hat with her lucky hatpin, and pulling on a pair of summer gloves, she was ready to set out for the day.

Her weekly column was due, and she wanted to talk with Max, the *San Diego News-Herald's* assignment editor before he started on his Tanqueray. Max generally kept his gin drawer closed until

Noon. But sometimes his drinking began early with his morning coffee, black and steaming hot, which arrived on his desk courtesy of Lucy the receptionist.

Leaving her motorcar parked in the gravel lot behind her apartment building, Sadie walked half a block to the trolley stop. She was far too practical to drive her Model T when, for a few pennies, the trolley could drop her off directly in front of the *Herald's* downtown building.

Feeling the morning chill, Sadie thought of her boyfriend, Roger, still snug in bed. San Diego's most eligible bachelor, Roger Siebert, was charming, good-natured and handsome. She pictured him sprawled in his gray silk sheets and felt a moment of envy.

But she intended to become a famous investigative reporter like her legendary grandfather, Equal T. Brown. That would take a ton of hard work. So sleeping-in was not a part of her life plan. The early bird catches the worm and all.

She took deep breaths of cool, crisp morning air and watched the yellow trolley come to a halt at her stop. Switching her leather folio to her left hand, and grabbing the handrail with her right, she jumped up onto the car. The snaps and crackles from the overhead electric lines as the trolley started forward made Sadie smile. It was going to be a good day.

* * *

Not far away, in his tasteful but sparsely decorated bedroom, society photographer Roger Winthrop Siebert snored softly under tangled sheets. A gray silk, down-filled quilt had slid off the bed during the night and lay piled on the floor. The walls were covered with the same gray silk, but a large Persian rug in front of the fireplace added color. Over the mantle hung a misty Laguna Beach seascape by artist and family friend, Edgar Payne. It was an experimental painting the artist didn't care for, but Roger loved it.

Isaac Buckley, Roger's valet, and all-around man gazed quietly at his sleeping boss. He wished he didn't have to wake him so early. Roger's bad leg had kept him up until the wee hours of the morning. But rousing his employer couldn't be helped. When the

San Diego Police call, it's not possible to suggest they phone back at a decent hour.

The SDPD had left Buckley with an urgent message to pass on. A body had been found at the Panama-California Exposition grounds, and Roger was needed as soon as he and his camera could get there.

Buckley walked to the window and drew back the heavy silk drapes. "Mr. Siebert, Sir. Sorry to wake you so early, but you are needed by the police at the Exposition grounds."

A groan escaped from under the sheets. "I don't believe it. Just my luck. Did they say what to expect?"

"A dead body, Sir."

"Would it be in poor taste for me to say people should have some consideration and plan their dying during proper daylight hours?" He poked his head and arms out, yawned and stretched. "Sorry Buckley. That was vile of me. I'll blame it on lack of sleep."

"Ummm..."

"Okay. I'm getting up. I'm getting up." He rubbed the stubble on his face and sat up.

"Here's your coffee and some toast. I'll start the shower."

"Thank you. You're a lifesaver."

"Ummm. I'll put out casual clothing, shall I? Last time you visited a murder site, I was obligated to toss out a new pair of spats. Blood is impossible to remove unless I get to it right away."

"Casual and no spats are perfect." The coffee was faultless, loaded with cream, and an ample amount of sugar.

As Roger showered and dressed, Buckley filled Roger's Harley-Davidson's sidecar with lighting equipment, a collapsible pull-cart, and a satchel containing the Graflex Century Graphic 23 camera his boss preferred for police work.

* * *

Most residents of San Diego were still tucked in bed and fast asleep, but others had to be up and about. Gleaming new Model-T delivery trucks and some soon to be phased-out, horse-drawn milk wagons rattled through the streets obliging Roger to keep to a slow speed.

The small, quiet town of his youth was becoming a big city. A building boom was underway in large part because of San Diego's 1915 Panama-California Exposition. The Expo was created (at great expense) in celebration of the completion of the Panama Canal. In return, the city expected fame, fortune, and tourists to follow. And they did.

Visitors to the Expo were taken by the delights of the city, the ocean, and the healthy weather. Many chose to move here. The city's movers and shakers were proud as the peacocks who roamed the Expo grounds. Roger wasn't quite as delighted.

It was a short ride from Roger's home to Balboa Park where the Exposition covered a hilltop. Except for the poor bloke in the Lath House, today looked to be another perfect day in paradise.

A police officer recognized Roger. "I was told you should go directly to the Lath House, Sir."

"Is Cohen here?"

"The coroner beat you by about fifteen minutes."

The officer waved him through the parking lot onto the grounds.

He drove down a broad boulevard, past the Spanish Baroque style exhibit buildings, spectacular fountains, and full-grown trees and flora which gave the illusion of an old Spanish town and plaza. The grounds were especially beautiful when the city was bathed in Southern California's crystal-clear sunshine. Today was such a day.

Leaving his motorcycle on the main avenue, Roger placed his satchel and equipment on his small cart and made his way through curious crowds to the Lath House, aka the Botany Exhibit Building, aka Botanical Building. The structure was a massive, domed conservatory built with redwood lath boards and filled with thousands of lush, exotic plants.

Roger showed his ID card to an officer guarding one of the entrances and stepped inside. Under the large central dome, bright sunshine fell through the slats and lay strips of warm light on the plant life below. The heady smell of gardenias and ripe bananas plus the sound of morning songs from caged birds seemed oddly cheery considering the grim scene inside.

In a far corner, a body was half-hidden under a giant coastal fern and a towering banana tree. Moving closer Roger saw it was a rotund, fortyish man. He was on his back and posed in a coffin-ready position...coins on his eyelids, pale hands folded on his chest, and feet, shod in perfectly shined shoes, rested on the pathway.

Coroner, Julius Cohen was writing in one of his ever-present red notebooks. He nodded at Roger and continued making notes.

Siebert set up his flash equipment and started shooting photographs. The sounds of the flashes and clicking of his camera were drowned out by the police tromping around and getting in each other's way.

Smoke and stench from the flash powder mixed with the odor of bananas and fluids leaking from the body. Not a smell one would want to bottle. Roger Siebert took his time and was thorough. He was a perfectionist, much to the dismay of some of his high-society studio clients.

Coroner Cohen smiled. "Just when you think you've seen everything, hey Roger? Laid out like that? Sending some kind of message I presume. At least he's fresh."

"I'm still not accustomed to photographing dead people fresh or otherwise. But then I don't have to tell these clients to stop fidgeting which is a plus.

"Isn't this pretty early for you, Julius? Why isn't one of your flunkies here taking notes?"

Cohen looked up from his notebook. "The police seem to think I'm the best man for the job because our body here is some famous doctor from Agnew Sanitarium. Suppose it's what I get for being the man in charge." Cohen ran fingers through his sandy hair and mustache.

"There are no apparent injuries, and someone posed him ready for the funeral parlor. Not your run-of-the-mill dead body arrangement. I like the coins on the eyelids...nice touch. The good doctor isn't staring at me while I make my notes.

"After all these years, I've never been able to shake the feeling the dead are judging me while I take my notes...demanding I don't miss the smallest detail. It's their moment in the spotlight, and they plan to take every advantage. Like a scowling schoolteacher watching over my shoulder while I take my end-of-year exams."

He read from his notes. "Doctor Asa Wolf. White male, age forty-five or thereabouts, overweight and looks to have maintained a very unhealthy lifestyle. Occupation: head of surgery and on the Board of Directors at Agnew Sanitarium and Hospital.

"No blood. No obvious trauma. If it wasn't for the positioning of the body, I would have guessed a heart attack. When I get him opened up in the lab and run some tests, I'll have a better idea of what happened to him.

"We've been asked to move him out of here as quickly and quietly as possible. Having a dead body in the park grounds is not the sort of publicity the Expo wants. Although there were six gardeners and a popcorn vendor gawking at the body when I arrived. No doubt half of San Diego is aware of every lurid detail. "

He watched a moment as Roger fiddled with his lights. "You look worse for wear, buddy. Late-night last night? Regrettably, pitching in for Officer Nelson while he's up north can mean any time of the day or night. Too bad because Nelson would have liked this one. He always likes the weird ones."

"I don't mind. True, I'm not keen on taking photos this early in the morning, but I did offer to help while Nelson's visiting family. But watch out. If he takes in San Francisco's Expo and sees the Kodak exhibit, I imagine he'll be requisitioning new cameras when he gets back."

"Fat lot of good it'll do him. I've been trying to get new lab equipment for over a year. And, it's not just my department. Look at the police, still using horses and a few motorcycles. They need automobiles. It's 1915, not the dark ages."

Cohen grinned at Roger. "Sorry for the rant. I can go on sometimes about budgets and the tightwads holding the City's purse strings."

He closed his notebook. "I'm finished here. If I don't see you before Nelson gets back from his vacation, it was nice working with you. Maybe I'll see you next time he takes a trip."

Roger nodded as he completed his last photograph. "You too, Jules. And good luck with the lab equipment."

Siebert packed up his flash equipment and camera as the body was carted out through the back exit past waiting gardeners. Thanks to the dead body, they were behind on their watering and weed pulling.

At the front entrance of the building, a police officer continued to stand guard and gave Roger a smart salute as he pulled his cart through the doorway.

Roger nodded at a group of maintenance workers across the way at the Home Economy Building. "What's happening over there? Looks like they have the entrance blocked off."

The officer scrunched up his nose. "Someone stopped up the toilets and the bathrooms flooded. Big mess. Bloody rags I heard. Some people put anything down a toilet. I myself prefer a good ole outhouse. If it was good enough for my grandparents, it's good enough for me."

"Right. Not a good day for the Expo. A dead body and flooded bathrooms will put off the visitors."

"Humph, there'll be plenty of tourists who want to have a look-see. People love an accident and a murder even more. Murder and mayhem attract more than flies."

Weaving his way through the crowd and the electric motorized, two-seater wicker chairs, Roger stopped at the far end of the reflection pond. He and a lone peacock watched a young police officer interview a large, stocky man.

"I keep telling you, my brother-in-law didn't have any enemies, at least not any more than any other dedicated public servant. Yes, he stepped on a few toes here and there, but who hasn't? Asa was a respected surgeon at Agnew Sanitarium and Hospital and well-regarded by the staff and the patients.

"My poor sister. I have no idea how she's going to handle this. Straight to bed with a double dose of laudanum no doubt."

Roger's leg begin to ache. Dragging a cart full of camera equipment in and out of the Lath House was setting off leg spasms. A ride directly back to the house for a hot bath and a pain pill before his lunch with the Mayor was in order.

Settling his lights, cart, and camera in the sidecar, he was grateful the Harley's balky step-starter came to life with the first jump.

Maybe there'd be time for a quick massage from Buckley. The man was worth his weight in gold. An excellent masseuse, a trained sous chef, and skilled auto mechanician. If a guy had to have a bum leg, Buckley made things easier.

CHAPTER 3

July 8, 1915 – Morning after the Murder

Doctor Lafayette Watkins followed the police to his sister's large, Irving Gill designed home. He wanted to be with her when the officer gave her the bad news.

Since her marriage to Asa Wolf, his lively, vibrant sister had become a fragile woman with delicate health. The death of her husband could be devastating. He wasn't sure how she would take the loss of her husband or to the role of being a young widow.

Louise Watkins Wolf received the police officer and her brother on the sun-dappled terrace where she was sipping tea and enjoying the hummingbirds zipping around her lush garden. The family's driver, an amateur horticulturist, had filled the garden with colorful, sweet-scented plants drawing birds by the dozens.

"Fayette, how nice to see you this lovely morning. Oh dear, this must be an official visit of some sort since you brought a member of the police department with you. A handsome member, I might add." Her smile was charming and innocent, as always.

Dr. Watkins had told a good many people bad news about their loved ones, but this was family. He didn't want to deliver the news to his little sister. However, he was forced to as the officer opened a notebook and looked over at the older man, waiting. Fayette Watkins grimaced and stepped up.

"It's about Asa. I wish there was an easier way to say this, but he's not coming home. He passed away last night."

Lou looked up at her brother and then down at her hands which began to tremble. "I don't think I understand, Fayette. Asa told me yesterday morning he would be having dinner with his Phrenology Study Group. The group always make a late night of it. I expected he'd sleep in his office at the hospital. The police must be mistaken."

Fayette patted her hand. "I know this is horrible and shocking, but I saw him thirty minutes ago. There's no mistake, Lou."

She sat frozen and scanned her brain for what would be the most appropriate response of a new widow. Both men assumed she was in a state of shock.

Her brother squeezed her hand. "Would you like some laudanum and a lie-down, dear?"

Her lips quivered and tears filled her eyes. "Yes, Fayette I would. In a minute. First, tell me what happened."

The officer, realizing he had appeared unprofessional earlier, stepped forward. "Well, umm, Mrs. Wolfe, your husband's body was found this morning at the Exposition, in the Lath House. At the moment we don't know how he died. So, ah, it's being treated as suspicious, to be on the safe side."

"Suspicious? No, no, no, can't be. Last year he suffered a heart attack and another attack the year before. That must have been what happened, a heart attack. Nothing else makes any sense. Or maybe an accident?"

The officer didn't comment. He tapped his notebook with a pencil. This wasn't going the way he wanted. Mrs. Wolf was creating her own scenario. On top of which, he felt uncomfortable in the presence of beautiful women like Mrs. Wolf. They made him stumble over his words like some vaudeville comedy act.

"So, umm, did he contact you at any time after he left yesterday? And what time was it by the way?"

He again lost control of the questioning as she jumped back to his use of the word 'suspicious.'

"Excuse me? Suspicious? Why do you say suspicious? Surely you don't mean suicide. It would be completely out of character."

She paused. "Or...murder? Murder? Is that what you are implying? Impossible! My husband dedicated his life to helping people. His research is...was...focused on helping people. He was respected. No one would want to murder him." Lou took her brother's offered handkerchief and dabbed at her eyes.

The officer cleared his throat and said nothing. Looking down at his notebook seemed best. Next time he would use the phrase 'looking into all possible causes.' Seemed safer than 'suspicious.'

Lou sniffled and dabbed at her eyes again. "Yes, well, to answer your question. Yesterday morning, he had breakfast...French toast, bacon and a cup of Earl Grey tea. He left a few minutes before 7:30 a.m. His usual time. He liked to arrive early at the hospital to prepare and not feel rushed for the day. And no, I didn't hear from him again after he left."

Fayette watched her and wondered how his sister had become a head-in-the-sand wife. Before her marriage, she lived life to the fullest, hiking, competitive tennis, and racing her motorcar up and down the coast.

All had been set aside for a marriage to a wealthy, older husband who virtually ignored her. It was as though she were marrying her father who, as Fayette thought about it, also never had time for her.

Now Lou spent her time finding the perfect piece of furniture to decorate the superb home Asa had purchased. She played bridge at the country club, joined a garden club, and took watercolor classes.

Each month Lou met with other respectable women from good families to help support the library. They called themselves volunteers but rarely entered the library itself. Their primary goal was to raise money through various society events to purchase books for the institution. They saw themselves as aiding those less fortunate.

The young woman who once craved fun and excitement was gone. She had become a staid, conservative matron who often complained of headaches and exhaustion.

It had been difficult to watch his sister sink into her role as Mrs. Asa Wolf. But there wasn't a thing he could do about it. At least their mother was happy. In her words, marriage had 'tamed her unruly daughter.'

Lou put a hand to her forehead. "This is completely beyond me. I can't make any sense out of it. Please, if you'll excuse me, I think I'll lie down now."

The relieved officer closed his notebook. "If we have any more questions, Mrs. Wolf, we'll let you know. Umm. Someone will contact you when the coroner makes his decision about the cause of death. His office will call to ask for the name of your preferred mortuary in a few days. Thank you for your help. And, ah, my sympathies."

Fayette took her hand. "Lou, do you need more laudanum? I can have a fresh bottle sent over."

"No Fayette dear, I'm well supplied."

"Do you need help upstairs? Shall I call your maid?"

She looked pained but shook her head.

"No? Then we'll let ourselves out."

Lou waited until she heard the officer's motorcycle roar down the street and then walked into the library. Behind a locked door of Asa's liquor cabinet, she removed a Lalique glass bottle containing outlandishly expensive bourbon. Pouring herself a stiff shot, she downed it and felt relief flow through her body.

Beth, the longtime housemaid, stopped her dusting. "Bad news?"

Lou poured another shot. "Asa was found dead this morning. How soon, do you think, before a grieving widow could in good taste unload this damn house?"

* * *

After the unhappy conversation with his sister, Fayette sat in his older Runabout. He watched the officer drive off the property and turn towards town and the police station. Taking a deep breath, he laid his head against the steering wheel and began to shiver as though someone had dumped a bucket of ice down his back.

The officer's parting comment had been, "I'm only a cop, not a detective. But having the body posed like that? Very unusual. Looks like murder to me, unless some well-meaning idiot found the body and posed him. It could have happened but seems unlikely."

Fayette whispered to himself. "Get a grip. This is just the beginning." His thoughts circled like a cyclone. 'It's going to be a total circus when this hits the papers.

Early this morning when his nurse said the police were calling about Dr. Wolf, he had wanted to tell her to lie and say he hadn't arrived yet. The police always made him nervous. Any authority figure made him nervous. He might have been named after Civil War hero, General Lafayette Watkins, but in reality, he was just a foot soldier full of false bravado.

So fraud that he was, he thanked his nurse and picked up the phone. "This is Dr. Watkins. How can I help you?"

"Are you a friend of Dr. Asa Wolf?"

"I'm his brother-in-law. Is he in trouble?"

"In a manner of speaking. A body was found early this morning at the Exposition. There's a good possibility it's Dr. Wolf. We found his identification badge from the hospital and one of your calling cards. Would you mind coming over to the Lath House to make a positive identification?"

"What? I just saw him yesterday. But, yes, of course, I'll take a look at the body, but maybe it won't be him. Right? Was it an accident? I mean, of course it was an accident."

"I wasn't given that information."

"Sorry, this has put me in a muddle. I'll be right over."

* * *

If the young cop was right in his analysis and the police decided the death was murder, they would be all over family members with question after question. First in line...Fayette and Lou, every aspect of their lives examined under a microscope.

15

He needed to keep his wits sharp as a knife. Too many secrets could unravel. Bad mistake not finding his personnel file before this happened.

He felt sick. But he reminded himself, the police would soon find Asa had an army of enemies and lived well beyond his means...huge house, expensive car collection, mistresses, trips, etc. All of which could point to any number of reasons for him to end up murdered.

Sitting in his motorcar, his mind took another path. Who, he wondered, would tell lovely Nurse Rose about the death of her illicit paramour, Dr. Wolf? She would undoubtedly need much comforting from a sympathetic friend, a friend such as himself.

More importantly, with the death of Asa, there was hope the Sanitarium Board would look to him to fill Asa's place as head of surgery. He was the most senior of the surgeons. Thoughts of a substantial raise and a new Packard Touring car made him feel almost normal again.

He set the gas leaver and the spark, stepped out and gave the crank a good swing. The solid roar of the runabout's engine always gave him a nice lift.

Thoughts of Nurse Rose and a sweet raise, maybe even a bonus, put him in a cheery mood. He jumped in the driver's seat, released the brake and put the car in gear.

Imagining the turmoil he would find at the hospital, he couldn't contain a nervous laugh. Easing out the clutch, he drove out of the parking area and turned down the hill towards the hospital.

* * *

Nurse Rose took the news of Dr. Wolf's demise with the composure of a saint.

"How awful. Have you heard what happened exactly?"

"No, but remember he had a heart attack last year?"

"Yes, I remember. It caught us all off guard."

"I hope it was something other than his heart. Heart attacks can be unbearably painful. And poor Mrs. Wolf. She must be terribly upset." Said the day nurse sharing the news with the satisfied tone of a town crier.

"Indeed," Rose responded.

Rose's fondest hope was a maximum amount of pain had been involved in Asa Wolf's death. Adjusting her face to show great sorrow, she took her clipboard and started her rounds in the massive room full of electric cabinet baths.

She checked a name on her clipboard and strode over to Mr. Fields who was creating problems as usual.

"I want out of this thing. I fainted dead away last week, you know. I didn't come here to be tortured."

"Mr. Fields, your doctor left specific instructions for you to remain in the cabinet for a full thirty minutes. You have ten minutes left. The idea is to produce vigorous perspiration. You're not quite there. Be a good boy for Nurse Rose, won't you? I'll have that special treat you like delivered to your room later." She winked at the whiny patient and wiped his sweat-drenched face.

CHAPTER 4

July 8, 1915 - Morning after the Murder

On a normal day, if you were to walk into the *San Diego News-Herald's* lobby, your senses would be hit by the thunderous sound of typewriters and an overlapping smell of stale cigar smoke and cheap aftershave but not in a totally unpleasant way.

Today, the *Herald's* newsroom was in a state of excitement, and the noise volume was sky-high. The body of Dr. Asa Wolf, head of surgery and a member of the Board of Directors at Agnew Sanitarium, had been found at the Exposition Grounds. Whispers of something irregular had begun to filter into the newsroom. It would be a sensational story if it turned out to be murder. That was yet to be determined, but one could think positive.

Sadie Brown dropped off the copy for her weekly column, "Flying the Skies," in the copy editor's inbox, and did her weekly check with the assignment editor.

"Mr. Tobias, my Underwood and I are ready to do a real story. Got anything for me?"

Max Tobias didn't bother taking the cigar from his mouth. But he did acknowledge her by way of looking over his glasses when he shook his head no. Before she turned to leave, he motioned her over with a discrete jerk of his head and a rise of his massive eyebrows. "You ask every week, Miss Brown. Every week I say 'No.'" He removed his cigar to tap its ash on the floor and leaned forward, "A little clue here. The boss has a thing about 'girl reporters.' Maybe he has mother issues. Who knows? But I do know for darn sure, the boss would shoot me if I gave you an assignment.

"No, don't sit down. Did I invite you to sit? No, I didn't. Okay, here's the deal, I like you...in a father-daughter sort of way, just so there're no mixed messages. So I'm gonna offer a little advice, and then we're done here. Find a juicy story before the other bloodhounds in town. Write it up, and personally hand it to the boss with copies to me, the Managing Editor and the Assistant Managing Editor. If it's good, I'll go to bat for you."

His brows rippled again. "Well? What are ya waiting for? Get your butt outta here." He opened the bottom drawer of his desk, the Tanqueray Gin drawer, frowned and shut it slowly but firmly. Taking a gulp of his coffee, he stretched and took another puff of his cigar. Looked to be a good day for once with a possible murder story worthy of running on the front page.

Sadie made it to the sidewalk before she allowed herself to grin and yell, "YES! YES! YES!" It didn't bother her one bit when people turned to stare. She only wished her parents and Grandfather Equal J. were here to offer hugs and congratulations for this small but exciting bit of encouragement.

* * *

Separating the city of San Diego from the Pacific Ocean, a natural peninsula of land had formed long ago. It created a bay and protected the city and ships anchored inside the inlet. The peninsula, called Silver Strand ended at Coronado city and was capped by North Island. Mecca-like it beckoned to vacationers.

Coronado city provided a full range of choices from casual tent-camping to the luxurious delights of the internationally known, first-class Hotel Del Coronado. At the end of the peninsula, and across a shallow expanse of water called Spanish Blight, was a swollen bit of land called North Island where two flying schools were located, Glenn Curtiss Flying School and the combined US Army and Navy school.

The white, seven-story Hotel Del Coronado and its adjoining cottages with their red roofs sprawled across a large section of the small city of Coronado. For summer vacationers who couldn't afford a room in the pricey hotel or the cottages, Hotel Del constructed a mini-city of tents, restaurants and amusements with the same but less expensive amenities of the hotel itself.

Inside the hotel, everything breathed upper-class, Beach-Victorian panache. The ranks of the world's high and mighty visited assured they would be pampered like the demi-gods they were...or as they no doubt perceived themselves to be.

Lunchtime in the hotel's Crown Room was always a well-attended but leisurely-paced affair. Those wanting a quick rushed meal were directed to the sandwich and grill shops by the salt-water pool or the beach cafes in Tent City.

Under a crown-shaped chandelier, Roger and the mayor, who relished long, relaxed lunches, enjoyed their meals of steamed clams and hot garlic bread. They were deeply engrossed in preparing a presentation for the Coronado Yacht Club. Both men had been rowers in college and wanted the yacht club to create and sponsor a team for an upcoming state rowing championship.

Using his bread, the mayor sopped up the last of the spicy clam broth from the bottom of his bowl. He wanted another order of clams and garlic bread, but his belt was already straining at the last hole.

"Our latest presentation at the club wasn't what you'd call successful. Fell flat as a pancake. Have any more ideas?"

"Yes, as a matter of fact. Let me pass this by you..." Roger and the mayor continued with the hatching of ideas until the mayor stopped their waiter with his biggest campaign smile. "May I have another order of clams, Reggie? Just didn't fill me up today."

"Certainly Mayor. I'll place the order immediately."

The mayor sniffed. "And mums the word about the second helping when my wife and her friends arrive this afternoon for bridge, righty-o?" What his wife didn't know wouldn't hurt her or bring on a fit of nagging. Besides, he's seen a handsome pair of suspenders at Marston's Department store. He'd stop by on his way back to City Hall.

The waiter gave the mayor a proper deadpan nod but added a cheeky wink.

Roger and the mayor continued with their plans, while tucked away at a far table, the last three members of the Francis Drake Historical Society were holding an emergency lunch meeting.

Member number one, handsome Simon Bennet had, as always, ordered the rack of lamb. The order required a 20-minute wait but 20 minutes nicely filled with alcoholic beverages.

Member number two, Jeffery, a large, florid man with a jet-black hairpiece put his bourbon down carefully on the table. "I don't think it's necessary to panic just yet. Asa said both the logbook and the map were in a safe place." He fondly stroked his remarkable beard. The facial hair contained two streaks of white creating a picture of elegance or an image of a skunk...depending on your thoughts regarding Jeffery.

Member number three, Ezra, a man with thin, wire-framed glasses and a nervous eye twitch picked at the napkin on his lap. "No doubt they're safe, Jeffery. But where are they exactly? What good does it do us if we don't know where to find them? There's going to be questions and pressure from the museum. If we can't find them, I absolutely refuse to deal with that loathsome Professor again. He may be brilliant, but he makes my skin crawl just thinking about him."

Simon, brushed a speck of lint from his Italian suit, pulled out a gold cigarette case and lighter. "I shouldn't worry, Ezra. The museum asked for more time to discuss the purchase price with their Board of Directors. Next meeting is two months from now. We have plenty of time to locate the book and the map. I'm not worried."

He lit a custom cigarette and blew a perfect smoke ring. "My guess is Asa has both the book and the map squirreled away in his library. I intend to stop by his house in a few 'respectful' days and deftly bring up the subject of Asa's library with his widow. How as Asa's good friend, I'd be happy to take on the task of cataloging his books. She's aware the collection contains some expensive first editions. Undoubtedly, it will be a relief for someone she trusts to take on the job.

"Knowing Mrs. Wolf, a quiet visit after the funeral won't be displeasing. She's not an innocent. I'm sure she's taking widowhood quite well. No throwing herself on her husband's grave and such theatrics. I can picture her right now happily going through Asa's financials and looking for a rich buyer for that huge house of theirs."

He pulled on his cigarette and released another smoke ring, as perfect as the first. "Louise Wolf and I go way back."

Ezra pursed his thin lips, pushed his glasses up and sneered. "Of course you do, Simon."

Simon leaned back in his chair. "Ah, here comes our lunch."

* * *

The police appeared at Agnew Sanitarium after lunch had been served and the dishes cleared away, but the smell of cabbage and mutton still lingered. The Chief had directed his men to be discrete and respectful. Compliance with his orders had lasted a good five minutes.

Every employee on duty and every patient who knew Dr. Wolf was questioned. It was obvious people found the doctor to be brilliant but lacked bedside manner. He was generally brusque and rude to his associates, underlings and patients alike.

Dr. Sanders provided the names of the men in the Phrenology Study Group, who met for dinner with Wolf the previous night.

An officer with prominent brow ridges took notes and tried not to wonder if Dr. Sanders would notice his forehead. Someone had once told him the shape of his brow was the sign of a dullard. Phrenology was an unproven science his wife had assured him. Sometimes he wasn't so certain. Fortunately, the doctor was busy preparing for his hospital rounds and barely glanced at him.

"Dr. Sanders, would you please tell me what happened last night when your study group met?"

"Well gosh, first we arrived at the park early to watch that Tiny Broadwick gal jump from an aeroplane with a parachute. From 3,000 feet I heard! Took my breath away. A girl? Can you imagine? Then, as usual, we met at the Tokio Café Chop Suey

Parlor on the Isthmus, you know the fun-zone at the Expo? The Ferris wheel, Sultan's Harem, and all? I always get the pork-fried rice. Kind of stuck in a rut. Find something you like, you know?" Sanders flipped through papers and made notes.

"Do you remember what Dr. Wolf ate?"

"Sake, lots of sake, lots and lots of sake." He laughed. The officer didn't. He was dead serious, all business. Sanders cleared his throat. "You probably mean food though. He tried a new dish. Something with octopus. Personally, I'm not a big fan of seafood, but Asa liked it. It amazed me how he could taste anything because he would heap dried fish flakes and crushed red chilies on everything, you know? How can you taste your food with all the chili and stuff? It's a wonder he had any taste buds left. Should have burned away long ago."

"Do you recall anything unusual happening?"

"Well, let me see. All went normally until the argument began."

The officer perked up. "Argument, what argument?"

"An old argument, you know? Patrick, Dr. Patrick O'Brien? His father had just received a letter from the Committee for the Betterment of the RMS Titanic Survivors? His father was once again denied membership. Neither the White Star Line nor any of the rescue ships listed his father's name dead or alive.

"The Committee didn't straight out say Patrick's father is lying, but it's implied you know? This leaves his father without an excuse for his long-overdue return to San Diego after visiting England.

"Asa, being his usual snide self, reminded Patrick of their bet and wanted to know when Patrick was going to dress up like a clown and ride up and down the Isthmus on a jackass. Well Patrick, being Patrick, became livid. He jumped up, face red as Hades, you know?

"I thought for a second he was going to punch Asa, who would deserve any number of wallops for his constant crass comments. But, no, Patrick gulped down his drink and stalked out of the restaurant."

The officer asked, "And Dr. Wolf's response?"

"Asa just snorted and lit another cigar. He was something, that Asa, you know?" Dr. Sanders leaned back and rubbed his eyes. "Sorry, a bit of a hangover. Anyway, afterward, as usual, we strolled about to take in the sights." He winked. "The dancing girls at 49 Camp and the Sultan's Harem on the Isthmus, you know?"

Not receiving an acknowledgment of any kind from the officer, he stumbled on. "After an hour or so, we called it a night. A little early as a matter of fact. Wolf was acting rushed. He'd found a note in his coat and kept reading it and smirking. 'A nice surprise from home.' He said.

"My driver drove me home. You can check with him and my wife if you need the exact time. When I left, Asa was walking down the Isthmus. He looked happy as a cat expecting a fresh bowl of milk.

"If there are no more questions, officer, please excuse me, I need more coffee before my rounds."

Dr. Patrick O'Brien was just leaving one of the four operating rooms when the police questioned him.

"Yes, there was an argument. The man always knows how to get my dander up. I suppose I should say 'knew.' But after I left the café, I took the first trolley home and spent the rest of the evening listening to records and playing Parcheesi with my wife and mother-in-law. You may check with them if you feel it's necessary."

The officer looked at his notes. "What did the study group do after you left?"

"I suppose they ambled over to watch the dancing girls as usual. But I wouldn't know now would I?" He shook his head as he dressed in a clean surgical gown. "Idiot," he mumbled.

When the officer asked if anything out of the ordinary had happened besides the argument, Dr. O'Brien became more than a little testy. "No, I did not see or hear anything out of the ordinary. Now if you don't mind. I need to get on with my next operation. Good day, Sir."

After questioning the patients and staff, the police promised to return in the early evening. Another group of workers, mostly nurses would be coming to work the late shift.

CHAPTER 5

July 9, 1915

San Diego's US Grant Hotel was a prestigious establishment built in 1910. It was situated downtown with a trolley stop immediately in front of the lobby doors. Adjacent to the hotel was the world's first electrically lit fountain, a meeting place for friends, family, and lovers. At night the first-class hotelery was so brightly lit it made one wonder about their electric bill.

If you wanted to make an impression, this was the place to be. And the Women's Press Club's Annual Scholarship Fund Auction wanted to impress and attract the people with the big bucks.

Roger Siebert sat in the lobby waiting for Sadie. Right on time, she sailed through the massive front doors followed by a burst of cool night air. Her crème silk gown and over the elbow gloves had been created by the talented hands of Mrs. Siebert's dressmaker. The dress had simple lines and designed without beadwork so it wouldn't detract from the bracelet she would be wearing for the auction, a diamond and sapphire bracelet that would be the highlighted item of the auction.

"You look beautiful, Sadie. You'll be the belle of the ball, you and the Tiffany bangle."

Sadie laughed. "Can't wait to put it on and flash it around the room. The club hired a security guard just for tonight to keep an eye on me and the bracelet."

In the top floor ballroom, they spent time before dinner and the auction talking with friends and discussing the war raging in Europe, the latest in photographic equipment, and the Glenn Curtiss Flight School. The school was Sadie's favorite topic. She was taking flight lessons and was giddy about it all.

A new arrival hearing the conversation stopped to ask, "So what did you make of Lincoln Beachey's crash in the San Francisco Bay? Doing a loop or something at San Francisco's Exposition?"

Sadie took a deep breath. "Truly sad, especially for the flying community. He was a great guy, but he may have taken the title of *The Man Who Owns the Sky* a tad too seriously."

She looked at Roger. "Flying is perfectly safe if you put safety first."

She smiled at the group around her. "I interviewed Lincoln a while back for my newspaper column. Fascinating man. Orville Wright said. 'An aeroplane in the hands of Lincoln Beachey is poetry.' I agree."

The man looked smug. "I heard he didn't die from the crash. He drowned. Trapped under the water for over an hour, they say. Doesn't own the sky now."

Sadie's immediate instinct was to tell the dreadful bore what he could do with what he heard. Instead, she reminded herself why she was attending the charity event and smiled. "Yes, I suppose it's true. So may I ask? Did you bring your checkbook?"

She lifted her wrist to show the Tiffany diamond and sapphire bracelet she wore which was the major auction item.

"Isn't it lovely? Ten perfectly matched diamonds surrounding a large, 3-carat Ceylon sapphire. Another lady is wearing the matching earrings. I hope they bring a good price. The Press Club's scholarship program is looking to sponsor more young writers."

The bore took a sip of his Isolabella cocktail and sniffed. "Yes. Interesting. Excuse me. I see a business acquaintance I must speak with."

His comments left a chilled atmosphere, but it warmed up when the group's conversation moved on to the gossip surrounding Doctor Wolf.

"Asa Wolf was a terrible braggart after a few drinks. And, he made a lot of enemies on his way to becoming head of surgery at the hospital. I imagine the police will have a long list of suspects if they decide his death was more than a heart attack. I've heard rumors of death by foul play."

"I always wondered where his money came from. Looked like he lived well beyond his means. You can't live that high on the hog on a surgeon's salary. Something was going on."

"I heard he owned railroad stocks."

"To give the devil his due, I understand Wolf was an outstanding surgeon."

"I heard that too. He operated on my partner last year and did an excellent job of it."

"Supposedly, he was a big-time expert in the field of female hysteria."

"He helped my sister's hysteria. One visit and she never needed or wanted a second appointment."

Sadie was about to make her thoughts known regarding the diagnosis called 'female hysteria' when a new arrival stepped into their circle.

He stretched out his hand for shakes all around. "Simon Bennet with the Francis Drake Research Society."

He smiled handsomely at Sadie. "Are you the lucky gal wearing that exquisite bracelet we all want to bid on?"

She held up her hand so he could look closer at the bracelet. "My oh my, Miss Brown. It's quite beautiful. I do hope it ends up on the wrist of someone charming and not stuck in a vault. Not where something so lovely should reside."

He smiled at Sadie and wiggled his eyebrows eliciting a laugh from her and Roger.

"Say, aren't you Roger Siebert the famous photographer?"

"No. No. Well yes, I'm Roger Siebert, but I'm not a famous photographer."

"You are much too modest. I've seen your work before. Quite striking. And didn't someone tell me? Yes someone did. You work for the police department from time to time. Not to be too nosey, but did you photograph the unfortunate incident at Balboa Park this morning? I heard he had a book gripped in his hands."

Roger tilted his head at the strange turn of questions. "I'm afraid Mr. Bennet I'm not at liberty to divulge information regarding my work with the police. But I can tell you, there was no book at the scene when I arrived."

"Ummm..." Simon lit a monogrammed cigarette with his gold lighter. "Please, excuse me. I see my friend has just arrived. It was a delight to meet you all. Do hope the bracelet fetches a good price. We need more well-educated young people, actually well-educated people in general." Simon turned and made his way across the room.

Sadie laughed. "Well, he was a strange one."

Roger nodded. "A bit creepy and too inquisitive for my taste."

The mayor and his wife soon joined their group. The mayor's wife hugged Sadie. "Sadie dear, your column last week was outstanding. If I was 30 years younger, I'd be taking flying lessons with you. And, I love what you have done with your hair. I'm not nearly brave enough to cut mine off as you did, but how liberating it must be."

Ever the politician, the mayor nodded. "Righty-o, Sadie. I like to see women stepping out of society's strictures...to a certain degree at least."

His wife took Sadie's hand. "Now, let's see that glamorous bracelet we've been hearing about."

* * *

Next to the bar in the back of the ballroom, the three men who comprised the Francis Drake Research Society drank cocktails. Two of them were asking Simon worrisome questions. The band arrived and began tuning their instruments.

Simon tapped his ear. "Let's go down to the Palm Court. Can't hear myself think in here."

The elevator whisked them down to the open-air Palm Court level. Smoking cigars and sipping their drinks, the men stood by the railing and looked out over the city.

Below, a trolley stopped to unload passengers in front of a movie theater showing *Birth of a Nation*. There was a line waiting to purchase tickets. D. W. Griffith's movie continued to play to good-sized crowds.

Simon flicked his ashes into one of the many pots containing palm trees. "So what did you two want to talk about? I thought we had everything settled at lunch today."

Jeffery ran his fingers through his beard. "I invested a good amount of money in this venture, money I can't afford to lose. The unknown whereabouts of the logbook and the map won't help my insomnia. So much tossing and turning, my wife already makes me sleep in the spare room."

Ezra nervously picked cat hair from his sleeve. "As much as I dislike the Professor, maybe it would be best if we contacted him and start again. Just a thought..." He glanced at Simon and looked away.

Simon allowed his usual good-natured features to twist into a show of dark irritation. "I said I would visit Louise Wolf in a few days and convince her to let me inventory Asa's library. That's exactly what I plan to do. After I search the library and if necessary the house, we'll meet again. I fully expect to have the book and map in hand. If I don't, we'll discuss our next step then and not before."

His eyes were black as night as he glared at both men. The next words were spoken in a calculated low growl. "Any problems with that? If so, let's hear them."

Neither man said a word, but Ezra's twitching eye was jerking overtime.

Simon's face slipped back into its customary, charming features. "Good. Let's go back to the ballroom. Dinner is most likely being served, and I don't want to miss the first course."

* * *

As the apple croquettes were served, the auction began. The Tiffany bracelet, matching earrings, and ten other donated items sold far higher than expected.

Sadie was thrilled. There were two young women she wanted to recommend for scholarships. Both women were talented and dedicated to their writing, but their families were financially unable to help them with books and university fees.

It was close to midnight when Roger and Sadie arrived at the Siebert house. Buckley ran a hot bath for them, placing lighted candles around the room.

"I've left champagne for Sadie and pills for you Roger. Remember Sadie, gentle massage, but not too gentle. I'll leave you to it, shall I?" He nodded and closed the door on the two lovebirds.

As much as Buckley enjoyed his job as Roger Siebert's all-around manservant, it was nice to spend a quiet night and not be "on call."

CHAPTER 6

July 15, 1915

Coroner Cohen's autopsy determined Dr. Asa Wolf had died from a heart attack. No sign of foul play could be found. No bullet hole, no knife wound, no contusion caused by contact with a hard object. There was some bruising, but a fall to the ground could be the culprit.

He ran tests from his regular list of poisons but found nothing. He searched for a fine puncture wound caused by an injection. Cohen started with the common sites and ended with the bizarre, once again nothing. Not even a mosquito bite.

Cohen gave a written and verbal report to the police department.

"All I can come up with is 'Probable cause of death due to a heart attack.' His heart was in terrible shape, like a tired balloon waiting to burst. Appears he'd suffered at least one major attack before. I'd guess he had numerous small attacks over the years. The liver was in crisis too. Too much alcohol consumption. Didn't take care of his health and a stressful job? Surprised his heart kept going this long.

"If the contents of his stomach were any indication of how he generally ate, it's a wonder he didn't have massive ulcers. The amount of red chili peppers in his gastrointestinal tract was amazing.

"Now the positioning of the body is a problem. Makes no sense no matter how one looks at it. If someone was trying to tell us something, darned if I know what it is. The gardeners who found him were adamant they had not posed the body in a misguided sign of respect. It's a loose-end the police will have to attend to. Not my bailiwick.

"For now, I'm not signing off on the death certificate until it gets cleared up. I've never liked reissuing corrected certificates. Makes my office look unprofessional. We don't rush things. I take pride in putting in the time needed to make a correct diagnosis the first time around.

"Mrs. Wolf is, of course, unhappy with my decision. Can't blame her. The family attorney contacted me and said the insurance company doesn't intend to pay any funds until I make a final decision. Wolf's policy has several exclusions including death by homicide and by suicide.

"However, none of this will keep me awake at night. The attorney assures me Mrs. Wolf is financially well off. With a roof over her head and food on her table, I refuse to feel pressured."

* * *

If the deceased had been some anonymous Joe from the streets with no family to protest, the police might have let the paperwork molder in the back of a file cabinet. But in this instance, the man had been a well-known and respected surgeon and researcher.

The underfunded and understaffed Police Department approved a two-man team to review all the evidence again, look at everything with new eyes. The Department didn't need or want accusations about lax police work.

With this in mind, the team asked Roger to come to the Department and go over his photographs with them. They hoped his memory would be jogged by some seemingly insignificant, but important item.

Documents and photographs were laid out in a tidy row on a conference table, and the smell of freshly brewed coffee greeted

Roger as he entered the room. Sergeant Evan Greenway and Coroner Cohen rose when Roger arrived. Officer Henderson was already standing next to a window. His expression made it plain he'd rather be elsewhere.

Cohen made the introductions. "Roger. Good to see you. This is Sergeant Evan Greenway and Officer Bartholomew Henderson. Greenway's heading up a two-man team to review the evidence we have regarding Dr. Wolf's death. He agrees with me; a killer was at work."

Henderson shook Roger's hand. Officer Henderson was unable to cover his boredom, not that he was trying. "First, the name is Bart. Second, if I may express my opinion, this whole review is a complete waste of time. We should be pounding the streets looking for the real bad guys, the muggers, the thieves, drunks..." He pulled at the ends of his old-fashioned handlebar mustache.

He looked at Greenway and muttered under his breath, "But no one ever listens to me."

Henderson was clueless. If he had bothered to ask, several men in the department would have been happy to offer the facts. Henderson's co-workers found him to be full of useless ideas, none of which ever amounted to a hill of beans. Even the horses refused to listen to him.

Sergeant Greenway smiled as he shook Roger's hand. "It's good to meet you, Mr. Siebert. Pour yourself a cup of coffee, and let's go over your photographs. They're excellent by the way. I'm hoping they'll jog your memory about some small detail. There might be something we overlooked."

Evan Greenway was probably the best man in the department to head up such a team. He thrived on detail and loved nothing better than solving puzzles, the more convoluted and difficult the better. While the other men in the SDPD were relieved they had not been chosen for the team, Greenway was delighted.

Roger asked about something that had been bothering him. "Off-topic, but I've been wondering, does the department have any idea why a murderer would pose Dr. Wolf? What motivates someone to do that?"

Greenway looked up from refilling his coffee. "Posing is unusual, but not unknown. Killers motivated by jealousy or rage sometimes leave their victims in ungodly poses.

"On the other hand, the 1890's Seaside Stiletto Killer almost seemed respectful. The killer left bodies, all seafaring men, on beaches from Oceanside to San Francisco. Each had been stabbed with a stiletto knife. The victims were found dressed in bathing attire and laid on towels above the high-tide line. Always posed as though asleep."

Roger was astonished hearing the gruesome information. "How terrible."

"The mind of a serial killer is dark and unknowable, Mr. Siebert. I've heard some of their explanations for multiple murders, but they don't ring true. In my opinion, that sort of killer enjoys mind games almost as much as killing.

"There may have been more victims, but we only know of five. The killer appeared to stop by 1898 and was never identified. Ideas as to why he killed and why he stopped are varied. None of which got us any closer to finding the slayer."

Roger tried to erase the images from his mind. "Those poor victims and their families. Sad business."

"Have you read Dr. Sigmund Freud's writings?"

Roger shook his head. "No, I haven't."

Henderson rolled his eyes. "Siggy Freud's a nutcase."

Disregarding Henderson, Greenway explained. "Dr. Freud has an interesting theory that could apply to killers and the reasons they murder and position the bodies of their victims. Look into his writings if you're interested."

Henderson snickered. "Freud and his ilk live with the fairies, as my old granny used to say. Let's get back to what we're here for, Sergeant. Which again is idiotic, in my view, 'cause we're just spinning our wheels going over the same old evidence again. We've already been over these photos and the facts a million times.

Henderson smoothed his mustache. "Talking to those self-important doctors Wolf worked with was a complete waste the first time around. Hope you don't expect me to do it all over again.

Besides, they all have good alibies. Except for wanting to party with the Isthmus dancing girls, they're blameless of anything as depraved as the sixth commandment."

"Opinion noted, Bart." Greenway handed out magnifying glasses. Each man took turns checking and rechecking the photographs.

Henderson picked up a photograph. "What's this glint over here do you think?" He pointed at a small flash of light some ten feet from the body.

Roger speculated, "Could be a piece of glass or maybe metal. Might be a good idea to drive over there and take a look...if it's still there."

Greenway nodded at Henderson. "Good work Officer. Good eye."

Henderson tried not to look pleased but was unsuccessful. His discovery would go a long way tonight when he told the story at Duncan's Bar. Might even garner him a free drink or two.

* * *

Roger wasn't officially invited along with the coroner and police to the Lath House. On the other hand, he hadn't been specifically told not to join them. Outside the station house, he hopped on his Harley and followed behind the police and Cohen.

Inside the Lath House, tropical plants soared above their heads. The air was moist and smelled of damp earth, fruit, flowers and other scents Roger couldn't identify. Caged birds chattered and people strolled about exclaiming over the exotic plants.

His eyes were immediately drawn to the spot where Wolf's body had been found. Surprisingly, he felt a twist in his gut. He imagined when he was much older and brought his grandchildren here, he'd have the same reaction. How did the police and Jules Cohen go about their daily lives passing by spots where ugly incidents had played out and not be reminded?

Coroner Cohen pointed. "Wolf was laid out here, and the flash of light came from over there." He walked over to the spot, leaned over and peered under a giant blood-red begonia. "I don't see anything that would create a flash of light, do you?"

Henderson leaned over to check the spot and straightened up coughing. "Holy Moly! What's that smell?"

Cohen laughed. "That, Officer Henderson, is the pungent smell of vomit. A common symptom of a heart attack but also a symptom of eating too many frankfurters and other tasty park foods. But after so many days, I couldn't determine if it came from the deceased or some child who ate too much popcorn.

"Ah, there is our flasher…a coin. A silver coin. Looks to be foreign, if I'm not mistaken. But once again, nothing definitive to tie it to Wolf. "

As they exited the Lath House, Cohen stopped and pointed at four large flowering plants growing on either side of the entrances. Their pale yellow, bell-shaped blooms were gigantic, and their sweet scent filled the air.

"That's interesting. Angel's Trumpet, a member of the nightshade genus. Quite poisonous. I missed them completely when I was here to examine and collect the body. Used the back door the day we removed the body.

"After I have my lunch, I'll go back to the morgue and perform some tests for that particular plant species. My practice of keeping bits of organs and blood samples comes in handy from time to time."

* * *

North Island was barren of vegetation except for some hardy plants which managed to grow in sandy soil seasoned with dried saltwater. A few buildings and a large number of aeroplanes and hydroplanes crowded next to airstrips and ramps built and maintained separately by the Army's flight school and the Glenn Curtiss School. From early morning to sundown, the noise could be deafening, but only the shorebirds complained.

Roger and his Harley took a ferry from Coronado to the Island and proceeded to the grounds of the Curtiss school. He parked next to the closest building.

Today he and Sadie had a picnic lunch planned. Wanting to try out a new camera, he had come early to watch her fly and click off some shots.

She and her instructor were in deep discussion. They were standing next to an older Curtiss pusher style aeroplane that Sadie favored. She preferred the open seating with the double wings and the engine & propeller behind her.

The school had newer aeroplanes with enclosed bodies and engines located in the front, but Sadie said she felt more comfortable with the "pushers," so-called because the engine pushed the aeroplane. She particularly liked having the engine behind her. It kept the fuel and oil fumes out of her face.

Roger wondered if it also had something to do with being in confined places. She didn't particularly care for elevators either. He knew Sadie's parents had died when they were trapped in the collapse of a rooming house during the 1906 San Francisco earthquake and fire. He understood the deaths had a devastating impact on her including something akin to claustrophobia. She might never be able to put it behind her. But about her parent's death, he asked nothing. She'd talk to him about it if and when she was ready.

As Roger walked towards the two, he heard the instructor.

"Sadie, you are not ready to try acrobatics, even simple ones. Just go up, take a few turns around the island and land like a good girl."

Roger could almost see steam erupting from Sadie's ears. Telling her she couldn't do something was bad enough, but calling her a 'good girl' was asking for trouble. On the other hand, Roger agreed she wasn't ready for acrobatics, an opinion he'd keep to himself. Better to hold his tongue on the subject of flying.

Irate, Sadie climbed into the pilot's seat of the craft, and the instructor took several hefty pulls on the propeller. The Curtiss engine roared to life with a thunderous sound. Roger could feel the vibrations rumble in his chest as well as his ears. Sadie taxied towards the runway and was up in a cloudless sky before he knew it.

As suggested, she flew several rounds following the perimeter of the island and landed. Taxiing over to the main buildings she saw Roger, smiled and waved.

Just seeing Roger brightened Sadie's day. Her previous upset with the instructor was forgotten. Removing her leather helmet and fluffing up her hair, Sadie reminded herself how blessed she was Roger still found her attractive in spite of what her grandparents called, 'A disaster of a haircut.'

Last Sunday she had spent a long, trying Sunday dinner at her grandparents' home. The pixie haircut was just one in a long line of criticisms from them.

"What were you thinking? First, you take up the unladylike, not to mention dangerous, hobby of flying. Then you chop off all your beautiful hair so some sort of leather flying-hat fits. Goodness!

"We have no idea what you were thinking, Sadie. You'd better hope Roger continues to court you. We can't think of any other man who would put up with your shenanigans. You're becoming more like that grandfather of yours every day."

She wanted to say 'Daddy would have loved it. And grandfather, Equal J., might have been notorious and a scamp, but he was a wonderful scamp.' But Sadie kept silent. Silence was the only way to avoid an argument and keep her sanity.

Orphaned at age sixteen, Sadie moved in with her maternal grandparents in their home in San Diego. After years of trying to voice her opinions and explain her actions, she gave up. Quarreling only made matters worse.

They had been trying to tamp down her exuberance from the day she moved in. Nothing they said or did turned her into the meek and malleable girl they preferred, but they continued to try. It was only because they loved their granddaughter and wanted her happiness that they tried to make her conform. It was something Sadie knew and accepted.

Sadie shook off thoughts of Sunday dinner. The sun was shining and she was joining her best friend and maybe husband one day for a picnic lunch in a park at Coronado. Even better, he had brought food prepared by Buckley.

"I've been looking forward to a Buckley picnic all morning. How fortunate you found him."

"Good timing I think. The day he quit, I was in the restaurant when a chef threw a meat cleaver at him. Fortunately for all concerned, he missed. Buckley didn't say a word, just calmly walked out the door and down the street. The man has nerves of steel with hands to match. I tracked him down, offered him a job. Easy as that. About as easy as you deciding you wanted to fly."

Roger spread out a blanket on the green lawn near the bay and opened the food basket. Sadie laid out the cream cheese and chutney sandwiches and a colorful shrimp salad.

"It wasn't that I wanted to fly, Roger. I had to fly. From the moment I first saw an aeroplane fly overhead, I couldn't wait to pilot one myself. Now it's something I could never give up. When I'm up there and see the ground sliding by below me and the sky above, I feel a thrill but also a calmness at the same time. Something I can't explain actually.

"When my parents died in the quake, it changed things for me. People don't always get a second chance. I have to grab life and take what I want before it slips away from me."

"True as the north star. Second chances are hard to come by."

As they ate, they watched people stroll through the park and enjoy the sunshine. It was a picture-perfect day. Halfway through lunch, Sadie pulled three Japanese postcards from her jacket.

"Ta-da! These were in the collection box at the charity store. I was going to surprise you with them for your birthday. But you know me. Delayed gratification is not my thing. Someone wrote on the back, 'Trial woodblock prints on postcards by Yokoyama Taikan.' Isn't he your favorite artist?"

"You remembered his name? That's impressive. Let me take a look."

Roger examined the cards, front and back. "This is his Hanko stamp. Remarkable! I wasn't aware he made woodblock prints let alone postcards. Maybe he didn't consider them worthwhile. Fantastic addition to my collection. Thank you!"

He gave her a quick but chaste kiss and hug which he thought was perfectly suitable in view of the public. However, two elderly ladies strolling past didn't seem to think so. He heard several "tut-tuts."

Sadie giggled at the reaction. "That should spice up their teatime conversation."

Roger laughed. "Some people can't adjust to the times. It is 1915 after all. Hope we don't get cranky in our old age." He stretched and leaned back.

"How did the flying lesson go today?" He didn't mention her argument with the instructor.

"Stanton is a first-class prig, but the best instructor around and knows his stuff. He also knows how to annoy me, but I have to admit he's always right. You missed our argument about me trying a few simple aerobatics."

Roger couldn't help but tread where he knew he shouldn't. "Fancy flying? Perhaps you're pushing things a bit fast? You have been known to get yourself into trouble by jumping into things before you're ready."

Sadie gave him a sharp look. "Okay I see his point about aerobatics, but I have asked as a matter of safety that he teach me the mechanics of pulling out of a spin. Landing unscathed is preferable to crashing. I think it's pretty important."

Noticing Roger's expression, she decided to change the subject. "Anything new on Dr. Wolf's death?"

Roger took a sip of his Dr. Pepper and felt relieved his comments hadn't started a quarrel but alarmed by the talk of a spinning aeroplane.

"No. Jules Cohen still has Wolf listed as a "possible" natural death by heart attack. But Jules says it doesn't sit right with him. There are several things which make one wonder what was going on at the time of Wolf's heart attack. Everything seems a bit iffy. Jules doesn't like 'iffy.' A good character trait for a coroner."

Sadie was folding the wax papers that had wrapped the sandwiches. Buckley liked to make his own with paper and beeswax. They were washed and reused. Never tossed out unless they became torn. Sadie reminded herself to ask him for a lesson.

"Probably doesn't mean anything, but Jennifer Ellsworth dropped a piece of gossip at the auction the other evening. Seems

Dr. Wolf had a habit of bedding the hospital nurses and then leaving them high and dry when he grew bored with them. As Jennifer tells it, Dr. Wolf forced more than a couple of his nurses to quit Agnew and leave town."

"Interesting. I'm assuming Miss Ellsworth didn't bother to pass this information on to the police?"

"No. She did not."

Roger made a mental note to make sure Sergeant Greenway was informed of this pertinent bit of chinwag.

Sadie finished the last of the salad and selected some of the grapes. "I hadn't realized how hungry I was. A good meal after flying is always special. Tell Buckley he made a masterpiece with this shrimp salad. Yum."

She leaned back and watched a hydroplane take off from the water. It wobbled a bit.

Roger thought it might be one of the new Army/Naval officers learning to fly. The pilot landed back in the bay, the sun sending sparkles of light off the water as it splashed up from the pontoons. He motored about to face the wind and gunned the motor lifting into the air again.

"Feel a little envious, Sadie, what with the Army and the Navy getting most of the air time since they purchased the new hydroplanes?"

"Sometimes. I only get an hour or two here and there where ever they can fit me in. But with the war in Europe spreading, our military will need aeroplanes and pilots if we get caught up in it."

"Let's hope that doesn't happen. Thankfully, we're a long way from the fighting."

Roger didn't like thinking about the war. If the United States entered the fighting, he'd be classified as 4F due to his bad leg. It was an unsettling thought. Watching his friends go off to defend the country while he sat on his rear end in San Diego didn't bear thinking about.

He decided to change the conversation to something lighter. "Back to the gossip. Did Miss Ellsworth mention any of the ex-mistresses by name?"

"No. Not particularly nice to say, but Jennifer's generally interested in passing on gossip, never interested in fact-finding or the truth. At least as far as I can tell.

CHAPTER 7

July 15, 1915

"Roger, darling, it's been ages." Mrs. Siebert, a small-statured but robust older woman, opened the door as her majordomo, Mr. Ito, was busy in the kitchen.

"Ages? It's only been two weeks, Mother. Remember we drove over to the Expo, had lunch at the Hawaiian Village, then dessert and tea in the DAR Tea Room followed by an organ concert? Quite the whirlwind." Roger laid two wrapped gifts on the entry table.

"Really? Two weeks? It seems much longer than that. I guess my memory is starting to slip. The joys of one's elder years are not as promised. Are you drinking tonight?"

"Yes, thank you. I could do with a nice glass of wine before dinner. You'll be happy to know I found the English heritage rose book you wanted. And I found a small portfolio of photographs taken in Kyoto for Mr. Ito.

"And speaking of Mr. Ito, what's he cooking up for us tonight? It smells delicious!"

"As if you didn't know...your favorite standing prime-rib roast, baked potatoes and Brussels sprouts with bacon. And for dessert, strawberries and cream over lemon cake. As usual, he's cooked enough for three men and a horse. I'll be eating leftovers for a week."

"Mother, I wish you would tell him not to cook so much when I come to visit."

"I've tried before. Never works. He just sticks his nose up and sniffs. Besides he cooks the perfect amount whenever I have regular company. Even when the British Ambassador came for supper. It's just you, Roger.

Ever since you had your bout of polio in high school, he's been overly solicitous about you. I never ate so much of his Japanese version of chicken soup as I did the year you got sick."

Roger laughed. "Mother, Ken Ito is a special person, but he works for you. If you ask him to cut back on my prime rib meals, he should do so."

Now his mother laughed. "You mean like how you give instructions to Buckley, but he ignores you and does what he think's best?"

Roger grinned. "Exactly." He took his mother's hand in his and they walked into the dining room. It was set for a casual dinner, but impeccably so. Mr. Ito was lighting the candles. He pulled the chair out for Mrs. Siebert and returned to the kitchen to bring out the dinner.

The standing rib roast was perfectly prepared as always.

Not that Roger was interested in the subject, but he asked about the garden club. The club was a safe topic of conversation. He wanted to steer his mother away from some of her favorite themes like working for the police department seems dangerous and on the seedy side, all my friends have grandchildren and I don't, how's your health, etc. But tonight the subject of the garden club was a big mistake. His mother was off on a tirade.

"Oh! You would not believe what the club has up their sleeve! We created a new rose hybrid which is wonderful and quite thrilling, but the name they want to register for it is beyond me. It took us years to perfect it and now they want to name it after an actress! Can you imagine?

"It's these young, upstart women who come from new money..."

"We come from new money."

"Don't interrupt! I bet your friend Eddie knows this, this...actress. I was told she makes movies for a film company in Los Angeles. Isn't that the kind of company your friend Eddie works for in La Mesa?"

"Well, yes, but the company and Eddie moved to Santa Barbara."

His mother waved her hand impatiently. "Don't interrupt! Lillian Gish is her name. A hybrid rose called Lillian Gish? I can't imagine what these women are thinking. I thought about giving up my membership, but in reality, I think an older, wiser head is needed to prevent these sort of idiotic ideas."

After strawberries and cream over lemon cake, they moved to the library. Roger poured a sherry for his mother who nattered on, but Roger had stopped listening. He found sipping his coffee and nodding now and then was all his mother needed or wanted. She certainly didn't care to hear any feedback or suggestions from him.

When she stopped for a breath, Roger stood. "Think I'd better be getting home. It's been a long day."

"Oh, how un-motherly of me, carrying on and not inquiring about my son's health. Are you feeling okay, darling? Are you taking care of yourself?"

"Yes, of course. My health is fine and dandy. But I had a full day."

After giving an appreciative Mr. Ito the portfolio and hugging his mother, Roger drove his Harley for the two-mile journey to his home. Slipping in between the sheets he smiled and counted his blessings. The fact he no longer lived at home with his mother was on the top of his list.

* * *

It was late and terribly dark when Nurse Rose Trigby, jumped off the 12th Avenue trolley and made a dash for her apartment. The streets were empty of people, but since Asa's demise, she had become paranoid. She told herself she was being silly, but she couldn't shake the feeling of being followed. Just who exactly, she couldn't say.

Certainly, there was her fear of being found out. But she had covered her steps carefully. And Asa swore no one knew of their love trysts...or her private and very old secrets. Only he did, at least some of them. She hadn't trusted him with everything in her past. People had a habit of using old sins against you when you least expected.

Once inside her small apartment, she locked her door and performed a thorough look around her three rooms and bath. The shower curtain was exactly as she had left it, and the tub contained only the rubber stopper chained to the overflow.

Under the bed, boxes of winter clothing left no space for hiding, and her closet contained only clothing, extra blankets, linens, and hatboxes.

The matchbook behind the bedroom door hadn't moved an inch. The apartment appeared to be precisely as it was when she went to work. She heaved a large sigh and allowed herself to relax a little.

The night was quiet, her neighbors asleep. The only sound came from the gas heater and stove which softly hissed as she lit them. The kettle still held water from the morning and gently sloshed and scrapped as it was placed on the stove. She lit a cigarette and flopped down on her overstuffed sofa watching the smoke curl up towards the ceiling and waited for the water to boil.

Pushing up her sleeves, she examined the red welts on her wrists. Finally, they had faded to a pale pink. Lee Chang's Aloe and Opium Lotion had helped a great deal.

The kettle whistled from the kitchen. Grabbing the kettle off the flame, she took an old gray mug painted with the words "Best Grandad" from a shelf. It was well used, had a chip on the base, and was beyond special to her. The mug had belonged to her grandfather. Rose used it when she felt the need for a comforting hug. Tonight was just such an occasion.

She added a little of Asa's exorbitantly priced bourbon instead of sugar. Steam rose up and carried the fragrance of alcohol and fire-scorched oak wood. Rose found it pleasing.

Returning to the living room, she eased down on the sofa, her legs tucked under her. The scalding hot tea required a lot of blowing before sipping. While she waited, she let her brain deal with some worrying thoughts.

How would Asa's death impact her job at the hospital? Asa had promised her a promotion along with a raise in pay, but that would most likely be down the drain. Worse, her job might be in jeopardy. Perhaps it was her imagination, but since Asa's death, it seemed some people at the hospital had begun to avoid her. She had always wanted to believe her affair with Dr. Wolf was a well-kept secret. But, to be honest, it might be wishful thinking. There are few secrets in a hospital.

She carefully sipped her tea, added a second shot of Asa's bourbon and lit another cigarette. Wrapping an old knitted throw around her shoulders, she closed her eyes and let her mind drift back to the evening of July 5th, two nights before his death.

* * *

She met him at her door. He wore a large grin and was weighed down with shopping bags and her favorite blood red De Resht roses. She hadn't a clue how he managed to find them, but the smell and the cool softness of the petals never failed to make her swoon.

One bag contained a package from his favorite butcher with two prime-cut steaks and a bottle of his favorite bourbon. The other shopping bag was labeled with the name of a New York furrier. Inside she saw two boxes, one big and one small. Both were tied with gold satin ribbon. If the big box was what she hoped it was, she would simply scream with delight.

"I see you eyeing the boxes. No peeking. They're for after dinner, my sweet. So contain yourself. Best things for last as they say."

He took her face in his hands, ran his thumbs over her lips and kissed her softly. "Today went on forever. I couldn't think of anything except being alone with you without a bunch of nosy Nancy's around. Keeping my mind on my patients today was near impossible."

"It was the same for me. I watched the clock like a hawk all day long." She hadn't, but this was not the time to be truthful with the furrier bag resting on her sofa.

"Are you happy with the new sofa and the bed? I told Shaffer's Furniture to send over the top-of-the-line. The davenport sleeper bed you had was impossible to sleep on. And shall I mention, quite uncomfortable when it came to indulging our sexual fantasies?" He chuckled.

Rose chuckled too, but not because of any sexual fantasies. She had bluntly asked the Shaffer's deliveryman if the furniture was the best they carried. They weren't. But she did admit the new sofa and bed were far more comfortable than the old sleeper bed/davenport she had been making do with.

Asa made for the Waterford glasses he had stashed in Rose's small bar cart and poured himself a large shot and Rose a small shot. "Shall I keep your drink on the short side as usual?"

Rose nodded and took the steaks & the flowers into the kitchen. "Yes, please. You know me. Any more than a small drink goes to my head and I get silly.

"I've baked the potatoes, and the rest of dinner is ready. The steaks won't take but a minute to cook. They look delicious. You spoil me!" Especially, she thought, if there was a fur coat in the NY furrier's box.

Asa grinned, sipped his bourbon and examined the new sofa. "The sofa looks nice...and comfortable. Hope the bed is the same. I have some new ideas I'd like to try tonight. A good sturdy bed will make them even better."

He walked into the kitchen with his drink. "Darling, I have some papers, I'd like to leave with you, if it's no bother. Inquiries I made regarding a new surgeon turned up a rather sensitive reply from a previous employer. It arrived in the mail today, and I didn't want to leave it at work. Do you have a place where I can store it out of the way?"

Rose felt her stomach flutter. She knew he kept private files on the doctors and the nurses at the hospital...especially the nurses. More than anything, she'd like to get her hands on her own file and read what her last employers had to say. Hopefully, they kept their word about a recommendation. She had certainly kept her end of the bargain.

"Of course, it's no bother. In my closet on the top shelf, there are some hatboxes. Grab the square one printed with the houndstooth check. It's from Bloomingdales. I made a false bottom in it to hide spare cash."

He called from the bedroom. "It fits perfectly. I don't see any spare cash though. If you're a good girl tonight, I'll see about a raise...or maybe a nice bonus...or maybe both."

He laughed. "There's a lot of hatboxes in here. You collect hats the way I collect first-editions. If tonight goes well and you enjoy yourself, I'll think about opening an account for you at Bloomingdales. How about that?"

"Don't I always enjoy myself? I'm not very worldly, but from what I do know, you're an incredible lover. World-class I'd say." She hoped she hadn't overdone the poop she was shoveling. He laughed, so he obviously loved hearing the poop, true or not.

"Dinner's ready. Would you pour the wine?"

Dinner was perfect. Cooked exactly as Asa liked. The roses had been placed in a vase on the fireplace mantle where Rose could admire them while they ate and Asa droned on. Dinner was a chore as usual. Asa was a meal-time bore.

She forced herself to appear interested as he talked about hiring a new surgeon, his research papers and his on-going fight with the U. S. Patent Office. He did get a little animated when he talked about the future marketing of an opium and cannabis-based cough medicine he was concocting. She was pleased with herself for not glancing once at the furrier bag on the sofa.

Eventually, he fell silent and coughed. "Okay, you've been sweet and listened to me rattle on since I arrived at your door. Now it's gift time. Open the smaller box first."

Rose felt her heart begin to race. "On my, Asa. I'm so giddy. Even my hands are shaking." She opened the box, pulled back the pale blue tissue, and giggled. "Oh, naughty black lingerie. How wonderfully sexy. Can't wait to see your face when I put these on."

"Now the big box."

She looked at Asa with expectant eyes. The same expectant look as Christmas twenty-some years ago when Santa left a doll-sized package for her under the tree. She hadn't been disappointed. It was the exact long-haired, blonde doll in the exact pink frilly dress she had seen in the window of Holcomb's Department Store. She had wanted the doll so badly, it was like an ache. That Christmas she was still young enough to think Santa had at long last decided she had been good and deserved her wish.

Asa leaned back with his bourbon and watched Rose as she took time to savor the moment. She let the satin ribbon slip through her fingers, slowly opened the box and pulled back the pale blue tissue. She gasped. A delicious silver fox fur coat was snuggled in the furrier box waiting for her to pull it out and appreciate its full glory.

Asa laughed delightedly. It never grew old watching his 'ladies' when they saw their first fur coat.

"Asa. It's so beautiful! The most beautiful thing ever." She meant it.

"That makes me very happy, my Sweet. Try it on. Make sure it fits.

"Oh no. Are those tears? Don't cry." Asa's face fell.

"Only a few tears, but happy ones." Rose was touched by his concern, a side of Asa she had not seen before. She reached over and kissed him softly. For the first time since her grandparents died, she felt cherished, loved even.

Assured by her answer and her kiss, he smiled. "What do you say we try something different tonight? Repetition can turn the best relationship stale as old bread. How about I go into the bedroom, you put on the little black knicker getup, the new coat and nothing else? I'll be waiting for you."

She shivered at the idea of wearing the gorgeous fur next to her bare skin. "Sounds exciting. A new fur coat and a new four-poster bed. Makes me feel like a princess."

"Princess eh? Maybe the princess would like a visit from a pirate wanting her private jewels?" He smirked, downed his bourbon and walked towards the bedroom removing clothing as he went. "I'll be waiting."

Rose grinned. Much like Dr. Jeckle and Mr. Hyde, after dinner, the boring Dr. Asa Wolf would switch to a sexy, imaginative lover. And Wolf, the lover, knew how to keep her wide awake and completely interested.

* * *

It was some night. But not the princess night she had expected. After he left, Rose fixed herself a cup of strong tea, lit a cigarette and lathered Lee Chang's lotion on her wrists. Red, angry welts circled her wrists and hurt like the devil and so did a few other parts of her body. So much for feeling cherished.

Fur coat or not, she needed to weigh her options. She liked a little kinky bedroom play as much as the next person, but Asa's requests were becoming distinctly darker. Rose was seeing a trend with Asa that could turn their enjoyable affair into something ugly and dangerous. Even though Rose had used their "safe" word, Asa had difficultly curtailing his desires. As she saw it, things were moving towards an unhappy conclusion.

Ending the relationship with Asa was one course of action, but it might mean losing her job, perhaps with no letter of recommendation. She admitted to herself she desperately needed this job. Her past mistakes had cost her. Finding another job would be monumentally difficult. But the situation with Asa needed to be rectified before something serious happened. Silver fox fur coat be damned. But could she bring herself to do what was on her mind? Rose opened the box of opium-soaked tampons Asa had left for her. She needed one after tonight's bedroom travesty.

* * *

Now a little over a week after Asa's death, Rose moved to her bedroom to remove her clothes and slip into warm slippers and her pink chenille bathrobe. The tea and bourbon were working. She felt her muscles relax. The bourbon was better than a steam bath and massage.

Back in the kitchen, she topped off her grandfather's mug. She was wondering what to do with the papers Asa had tucked away in her closet. Which made Rose wonder once again where he kept her file. She needed to see the letter of recommendation from her last employer...if indeed there was one.

Rose had been blamed for a sad happening at the Stockton State Mental Hospital, but that was due to the doctor in charge not wanting to own up to his idiotic mistake. At least that's how she saw the whole sordid event. A settlement was quietly made with the patient's family, and Rose was shown the door with an agreement to provide a good recommendation if she kept her mouth shut.

She hoped her file wasn't at his rumored private clinic. Lord knows where it was ...if there was a clinic. Asa always laughed off questions about a secret medical office hidden away on the outskirts of San Diego or, as some said, across the border in Mexico. Rose had long ago given up trying to decide when Asa lied or told the truth. It took too much effort.

Ever the pragmatist, Rose thought it much too late to worry about it tonight. Yawning, the box of opium-soaked tampons in one hand and her bourbon & tea in the other, she walked into the bedroom and called it a night. As she drifted off to sleep, a frightening thought crept into her mind. Did anyone suspect her of murder?

CHAPTER 8

July 16, 1915

Upstairs at the Wolf house, new widow, Louise Wolf was clearing out her husband's clothing. Unlike widows who keep their spouse's possessions until friends and family deem it unhealthy, Lou made plans to clear out Asa's closet the day after his body was found. In her opinion, unhealthy was creepy stuff like sleeping with Asa's old bathrobe for comfort or sniffing his shaving cream.

She was in his dressing room when she heard her maid answer the front door. The Salvation Army had said they would send a truck over Friday morning, so Louise assumed the driver had arrived to pick up the donations. The driver was earlier than she expected.

She yanked Asa's silk dressing gowns, hangers and all, from the closet rod and tossed them in a box. Lou had her hand on a wool coat when Beth, the maid spoke from the doorway of Asa's dressing room.

"Mrs. Wolf. Mr. Simon Bennet is here to see you. I explained you're in mourning and not seeing anyone socially. I suggested he come back next month and..."

Simon stepped from behind her. "And I said we were old friends, and I knew you would want to see me."

Lou slowly placed Asa's favorite wool coat in a box on the floor. Although she managed to appear calm, she was shocked and apprehensive. Was Simon here to start trouble?

"Simon. What a surprise. Why don't you let Beth fix you a drink in the library? I'll be down to meet you in a few minutes."

Simon smiled. "Still a sherry fan? I'll have one waiting for you."

"Just some lemonade for me, thank you." She nodded at her maid.

Beth gave a slight bow. "Yes, Mrs. Wolf."

Lou gently bit her lip and watched Simon turn and follow Beth downstairs to the library. Her hands turned ice cold. She reminded herself the one evening between herself and Simon, San Diego's biggest womanizer, was over and done with. Two years had past.

When she entered the library, Simon had a bourbon in hand, holding it up to the sun streaming through the French doors. Whether looking at the bourbon's clarity or examining the vintage crystal glass was made apparent when he spoke.

"Your glassware is beautiful. Waterford isn't it? Where did you find them? Waterford went out of business ages ago. Although, I've heard rumors someone is negotiating to purchase the factory."

"They're from my grandmother's collection."

He took a sip and held the glass to the sun again. "I love crystal. Beauty and fragility. A winning combination requiring delicate handling."

Lou wondered if there was a hidden meaning to the comment. She was probably being overly suspicious.

"Yes, they are fragile. Asa took six to his office and only four were found when his personal things were packed up. Not a big loss. My grandparents entertained on a grand scale and had dinnerware for fifty."

Simon removed a cigarette case from his vest pocket. "I'd offer you one, but as I remember, you don't smoke."

"Don't put them away. I recently took up the habit. So yes, please, I would like a cigarette. Beautiful case."

"It's new. Amazing craftsmanship don't you think? A novel design called Art Deco. I quite believe it's going to catch on and be the next big thing. A gift from an admirer." He winked and lit Lou's cigarette admiring her lips as he did so.

Beth handed Lou her lemonade and left the room. Lou took a small taste and hoped Simon would get to the point.

Raising her eyes to look at the always well-dressed and groomed Simon, she smiled. "Simon. I appreciate your attendance at the funeral. Asa would have been pleased. But I'm quite surprised to see you here today."

Simon assumed a serious expression. "You had quite a lot to attend to at the funeral, and we only had a chance to speak briefly. I wanted to offer my help, but it didn't seem like the proper time."

"Help? In what way?" her heart skipped a beat and her back stiffened.

"Any way I can of course. I don't have any ulterior motive. I promise I won't come on to the new widow Wolf if that's what you're thinking. I'm not that much of a cad.

"I'm actually here because Asa told me at the last Francis Drake Research Society meeting he was looking for someone competent to inventory his library. He asked me, but I said my calendar was too full to take on the project.

"However, my circumstances have changed. I'm now able to put myself at your disposal...to catalog Asa's collection of books...and anything else you need." He dipped his head in a courtly manner.

"How kind of you, but I'm going to contact Goldman's Fine Books. I'm told they're quite competent."

"Yes, they are. Also ridiculously expensive. Whereas I would charge you nothing. In truth, I owe Asa for the generosity he's shown me in the past. "

He gave Lou his most serious and trustworthy look. "If it wouldn't be too impertinent, I could start right away. I have three weeks free, and the inventory shouldn't take more than a week or two at the most. I need to be in Los Angeles by the 21st, and business will keep me there for some time. So it's now or never, as they say."

"I know you and Asa were good business friends, and he trusted you. And..."

"Speaking of trust, Lou, I hope you know, as a gentleman, I never mentioned our little *tête-à-tête*."

"Yes, I know, Simon. I appreciate your discretion. To be honest, that night, our night together, was a horrible mistake on my part. I drank too much and flirted like a fool with San Diego's most renowned Don Juan bachelor."

She thought a true gentleman wouldn't bring up their drunken interlude right after her husband's funeral. What the heck was he up to?

"It was a charming, unforgettable evening, but one I've kept to myself. I'm not known for bragging." Simon took another sip of his bourbon, frowned slightly, but then smiled.

Lou was pretty sure he could tell the bourbon wasn't Asa's special small-batch bourbon kept in the Lalique bottle. She imagined he felt a bit miffed. However, she was sure he'd keep a smile in place until he got what he came for.

She also knew Simon well enough to know he said nothing about their night together for one reason. It was an ace in his pocket for future negotiations. With Asa's death, the bargaining piece was null and void.

However, getting her husband's library cataloged and ready for sale had to be done as soon as possible. A large amount of money was tied up in Asa's books.

It was certainly possible Simon might try to pull the wool over her eyes, but she had Asa's list of his important first editions and rare books which she could compare with Simon's completed inventory. And he was offering his time and work for free. Greed won out over distrust.

"Thank you, Simon. You are a gentleman. I appreciate that."

"I do have to make a tiny confession. There's a small amount of money in it for me. A book collector I know has offered a finder's fee if I come across something he might find interesting. He would consider it a kindness if you allowed him to make an early offer."

"That works for all three of us. You should get some money out of this. It's a lot of work. Besides, I was dreading strangers taking up residence in my library. And as you and others have said, Goldman's would charge me an arm and a leg. I appreciate your offer, truly.

"On top of the desk is a list Asa made of his more important books and estimated values. It might be a good starting point."

The maid entered. "Ma'am, the charity collection people are here."

"Thank you, Beth. Have them wait. I should be finished packing Asa's things in another ten minutes." She turned to Simon. "When would you like to start the inventory?"

"How about now…if that works for you? I have ledgers and packing boxes in my auto."

"You came prepared. I'm not surprised of course." She sighed. "Best to get started, get it done and out of my hair. So today works for me too. After you finish here in the library there's the collection of Erotica in the wine cellar. Undoubtedly you are already aware of the cellar and its special library."

Simon nodded. "Yes, of course. Asa liked to boast it was the largest such collection in the state."

"Unamazingly, I've already had two inquiries about the collection. But perhaps your friend might offer a higher price."

"He might."

"The key for the cellar is in the liquor cabinet. Use it after you've finished the main library. While you're down there, you are welcome to a bottle or two of the wine in the cellar if you like. And, also, my brother borrowed some books just before Asa died. I'll have him get in contact with you."

* * *

Walking to the car to retrieve a large ledger book and boxes, Simon realized he had a job ahead of him. He had noticed several places in the library where a logbook could be hidden.

Asa had said he kept the map, the "supposed" treasure map, tucked inside the book. If he found the book, he'd have the map too. The treasure map was the all-important hook.

Hopefully, the cataloging wouldn't take long. The men of the so-called Francis Drake Research Society would be putting pressure to bear. And if he came up empty-handed, Ezra's suggestion to contact the Professor, was chilling.

The Professor was a brilliant craftsman, but difficult to deal with. To begin with, there was a language barrier. Besides, the guy had some nasty connections Simon didn't want to engage with.

Being a man of his word, generally, Simon would keep his end of the bargain and complete the inventory. He was, after all, a gentleman most of the time.

Besides, he looked forward to itemizing the erotica in the wine cellar. He particularly wanted to browse through the male art magazines without anyone reading over his shoulder and making snide comments. A glass of excellent wine and a leisurely read of magazines full of naked men in various poses was a heady mix.

* * *

From the upstairs bedroom window, Lou watched Simon walk to his highly polished, red roadster. Beautiful automobile. The man had good taste. She would give him that. But there was no denying he was an unapologetic rogue through and through.

He certainly wasn't taking time to inventory Asa's books out of the goodness of his heart or a finder's fee from a book collector. There was a catch. She just hadn't ferreted out what the catch was...so far.

* * *

Simon stood among the boxes and looked around the library. Considered a lucky man, he hoped his luck would come into play and the logbook would jump into his field of vision. He was well acquainted with the size and cover of the book. It was dark brown leather and stained with dirt and blood, dirt and blood he had himself smeared on the book. Unfortunately, he saw nothing that looked even close.

The contents of Asa's desk had not been noted as off-limits. While Lou was busy with the Salvation Army drivers, Simon quietly searched the desk drawers. Nothing. One bottom drawer was locked. Using skills learned during a stint in a San Francisco jail, the drawer opened easily. Disappointedly, only some file folders on various hospital employees were within. All female employees he noted.

Simon sat at the desk, opened a ledger and began to work. If he kept his nose to the grindstone, he should be finished upstairs in a week. After which, he could move down to the delights of the wine cellar. He didn't always save the best for last, however, in this instance, it was a prudent business move.

CHAPTER 9

July 23, 1915

In Asa's wine cellar a week later, Simon sipped a glass of Asa Wolf's finest cabernet and perused an illustrated book by the Marquis de Sade. He had searched every inch of the upstairs library and the wine cellar, checked behind paintings and any other hiding place he could think of, but to no avail. The logbook was not to be found.

The Francis Drake Research Society would not be pleased. But he wasn't worried. Plenty of time yet before the museum's board of directors met. If further efforts to find the book and map proved a failure, the Professor would be engaged to recreate another set. The man's work was incredible, the best. Simon would be forced to deal with him. Too much money was at stake.

The museum could be put off for a few months. They wouldn't like it, but it would also make them nervous thinking someone else wanted the book. It was a tactic he had used before which always worked in the seller's favor.

Surprisingly, he had been given access to the entire house while Lou and her maid were away shopping one afternoon. It was evident she felt there was nothing Simon would dare take. She and her maid had done a complete inventory of the contents of the house including the wine in the cellar. In a 'nice' way, Simon was informed the family attorney had a copy of the list.

As soon as Lou and her maid left, Simon performed a careful and thorough search of every possible hiding place. It was fruitless.

Time to finish up at the house and take a look in Asa's office at the sanitarium. Due to an ongoing legal battle between the Wolf estate and the hospital, the office at the hospital was locked and only the attorneys and hospital administrators had keys. But a locked door had never been a hindrance to Simon.

"Hello? Are you down there Mr. Bennet? It's Fayette Watkins, Mrs. Wolf's brother. I have some books for you."

Simon flipped the illustrated book closed. "Yes. Come on down. Join me for a glass of wine while I finish up the last stack of books."

Watkins made his way down the steps holding an armload of books. He was heavy-set, but even with his bulk, he moved easily and expectantly.

"I wanted to bring these by before I leave for a weekend in Redondo Beach. Goodness, I see you're about done down here." He sounded disappointed as he looked at the sealed boxes stacked on the long walnut tasting table.

"Yes. Didn't take long to catalog, even with the wine breaks...which your sister generously offered." He held up a bottle. "Would you like to join me?"

"If it's a cabernet, yes I would."

Fayette set the books down and poured himself a glass of the red wine. His mouth salivated. Asa only purchased the finest wines for his cellar. "Excellent wines in this cellar. Only the best for Asa." He raised his glass. "To Asa."

Simon raised his glass. "Yes, to Asa. A fine man, excellent physician, and with an expert's eye for great literature."

Fayette took a sip and made appreciative noises. "I can almost hear Asa. 'Scent of forest floor with overtones of tropical floral.' What say you?"

"Undeniably."

Both men drank while Fayette looked through the last stack of books yet to be inventoried and Simon checked and cataloged the borrowed books, all erotica.

"These are all the books you borrowed? Correct? No disrespect. Just dotting all the *I*'s and crossing all the *T*'s."

Fayette looked up from an open portfolio of French photographs. "Umm? Oh yes. Yes, quite so."

Simon noted a lack of eye contact and flushed cheeks. It takes a liar to know a liar, people say. And Simon was one of the best, liars that is.

"The reason I ask is your sister said you had borrowed ten books, and you brought back eight."

Fayette turned bright red. "Well, there was a Kama Sutra book and a book of Aubrey Beardsley illustrations Asa told me I could keep. Not first editions or anything."

"Just so you know, your sister has a list Asa made listing all his first editions and valuable books."

"In that case, there should be no problem. I'll let Lou know I was gifted the two books. If she wants them back, I'll do so, happily."

Simon smiled. "Perfect." He held up the bottle. "Have another glass of wine while I finish up these last books."

The final stack of Asa's erotic books was quickly added to the ledgers and boxed. Upstairs the men drank the last of the cabernet and chatted amiably about the war in Europe. They both hoped the country wouldn't be dragged into the fighting. All the while Simon watched Fayette closely for signs of deceitfulness. He didn't like what he saw.

"Well Fayette, I have to be off and research book prices. It was nice to meet you. Have a great time in Redondo Beach. Beautiful city. Staying at the Hotel Redondo?"

"Yes. It's my favorite place to stay when I want to get out of town." Fayette smirked. "And even better, the lovely nurse, Rose Trigby, has agreed to accompany me. Since Asa isn't taking up all her time, she's more than happy to let someone else treat her to trips. Delightful woman."

Simon faked a conspiratory leer. "From what Asa told me about Rose, you should have a most enjoyable trip."

Yes, Simon thought, Fayette was acting deviously. A search of Fayette's home over the weekend was in order and Rose's place too.

* * *

The ocean dashed against the shore beneath the three-story Hotel Redondo, and Bath House. It was a study in high Victorian architecture built on a bluff overlooking the Pacific.

In the room Watkins had reserved, Rose savored a second glass of Champagne. The first glass had gone a long way to relax her body and her mind. After leaving behind San Diego and the hospital, her worries and apprehensions lessened, but Champagne helped. She picked up a hotel brochure that had been left in their room and smiled delightedly.

"Fayette? Did you know there's a bowling alley here in the hotel? I'd love to give it a whirl. What do you think?"

"Sounds like fun." Fayette sipped his Champagne and stared out the window to the ocean below. Triple-masted ships waited along piers jutting into the Pacific. Railroad tracks had been built down the piers and a line of boxcars stood waiting while a manly choreography was performed of loading and unloading cargo and lumber. The little boy inside never got enough of watching the hustle and bustle of ships and trains.

Rose walked up behind Fayette and slipped her arms around his waist. "All the activity on the piers looks fascinating. I see I have competition."

He turned and kissed her. "Never in a million years, my sweet Rose. What do you say we have a bite of lunch and then check out the bowling alley?"

"Sounds perfect. I'm famished."

"Me too." He watched as she stood before a mirror and repined her new summer hat in place. "You're a beautiful woman, Rose Trigby. Thank you for joining me for the weekend."

Rose turned to see if he was making a cavalier remark. He wasn't. He looked perfectly sincere.

She smiled and slipped her arm through his. "It's my pleasure, Fayette Watkins."

They left the room, Rose thinking of lunch and bowling and Fayette thinking of neither. His thoughts were of the coming evening, the moonlight, the stars, and the joys of passion.

CHAPTER 10

July 24, 1915

With a set of convenient tools, Simon let himself into Fayette's apartment early Saturday morning. It was filled with comfortable furniture, a small but excellent library, a well-stocked bar, and a few good pieces of art. Over the fireplace hung an impressive landscape. He wasn't familiar with the artist, Laszlo Paal, but could recognize an excellent painting by a talented artist when he saw one.

Simon had underestimated Fayette's appreciation for the finer things in life. As opposed to many bachelor rentals, this one could easily be described as neat, tidy and dust-free. He wondered if there was a weekly cleaning lady or perhaps Fayette was obsessive about cleanliness.

He made a thorough search leaving all he touched exactly as he found it. Starting with the built-in bookcase, he checked for anything that could hide the logbook. Behind a collection of Shakespeare, Simon's deft fingers touched a secret compartment which echoed with a hollow sound. Inside, he found a stack of gold coins wrapped in a velvet cloth and a pouch containing loose diamonds. Even without a jeweler's loupe, he could see the diamonds were above average grade but not exceptional. A systematic search turned up nothing further. Fayette's apartment was a dead end.

Seven a.m. the following morning, he made entry to Rose's apartment. Early Sunday mornings were excellent for breaking and entering. People were happy to keep an eye out for burglars and water plants for neighbors who were away. But on Sundays, they liked to sleep in, sometimes until Noon.

After a book of matches slid along the floor when he opened the door into Rose's bedroom, Simon concluded Rose was one of those women who thought people were after her. Maybe they were. He thought her idea clever. The door had been left ajar with the matches inside near the hinged edge. A burglar in a hurry wouldn't notice, but Simon always took his time and noticed everything.

He found a letter of recommendation addressed to Asa in the fake bottom of a hatbox. A potential Agnew employee had been damned with faint praise by a Boston medical school. He had taught at the school briefly before he was asked to find another position elsewhere.

Rose had quite the collection of hats, but in his opinion, most bristled with far too many feathers and fake flowers. Before he could look further, someone began knocking at the front door.

A worried woman's voice called out. "Rose? Are you home early? Rose?" The knocking became insistent. The hair rose on Simon's neck, and a second of panic zipped through his body. But, number one rule for a person unlawfully entering private property, check all avenues of exit first.

Simon made for a screened-in drying porch off the kitchen with a door and steps leading down to an alley. He was blocks away before Rose's neighbor gave up knocking and went back to her breakfast and newspaper.

Maybe he'd give Rose's apartment another search while she was at work. However, on second thought, it wasn't likely Asa would hide something as valuable as the logbook at Rose's. The book would certainly be someplace where Asa could place his hands on it whenever he wanted.

Wolf's office would be next. A search late tonight would be perfect. The patients would be sleeping and minimal staff would be on duty.

CHAPTER 11

July 30, 1915

The weather for the Exposition's Japan Day was warm and sunny requiring hats and parasols. Roger and Sadie strolled about the grounds admiring the thousands of red and gold Japanese lanterns decorating the buildings and exhibits.

They had arrived in time to watch two Japanese aviators fly overhead and drop Japanese coins wrapped in red tissue. Delighted children laughed and screamed as they scrambled for the good-luck tokens scattering the ever-present pigeons. As the birds took to the air in confusion, Roger aimed his camera snapping photos.

Sadie looked surprised. "Won't the photos just be a mass of grey lines and swirls?"

"Yes. Should be interesting."

Sadie adjusted the ribbon on her straw hat. "Brilliant idea. That's one of the things I admire about you. Your approach to photography and to life is never mundane. I always wonder what you'll think of next. I'm so analytical. Wish I had even a tenth of your imagination."

"But you have the logical O&A which I find fascinating."

"I do, but I can't claim to have originated it. My father somehow passed it on to me. Maybe genetics. O&A...Observe and Analyze he called it. Sometimes I can almost hear him reminding me to use O&A. 'Look around you Sadie. What do you see? Think.'"

"Sounds like a good thing."

"Doesn't always work. There's interference from my grandfather Equal J. Brown's 'act before you think' genes."

Sadie adjusted her parasol. "Challenging a state champion sharpshooter to a duel certainly qualifies as an 'act before you think' foolishness. And the consequences ended Equal J.'s life on an untidy note. I'm a muddled mess at times."

"A mess I find fascinating. Besides your writing talent comes from Equal J. That evens things out, don't you think?"

"True. He was a famous journalist in San Francisco."

Roger pointed at a film crew. "I'm not the only one with brilliant ideas."

Recording every colorful moment of Japan Day were Panama Film Company cameras and crew members. Young women passed out red flyers to the onlookers.

****

YOU ARE INVITED!
WATCH Films of Japan Day and
Other Exciting Expo Events
***** PANAMA FILM COMPANY THEATER *****

Located on the Isthmus (close by the Ostrich Farm)

Relax in comfort

And enjoy your favorite piano melodies

****

Sadie laughed. "Look at that. Tourists taking photos of the film crew filming the tourists. Kodak must be making a fortune on film these days with the exposition here and the one in San Francisco."

"True. Wish I was a shareholder. Should we join the line forming at the teahouse? I'm ready for some tea."

The Japanese Pavilion's teahouse was overflowing with visitors...tourists and residents alike. Roger and Sadie waited their turn in line and were soon enjoying green tea, sweet rice cakes, and almond cookies.

Sadie, in an unladylike manner, licked her fingers after popping the last little cake in her mouth. "Yum. So delicious. I've tried making these myself, but they never taste this good."

"Mr. Ito makes excellent ones. Next time we have dinner at Mother's, we'll ask him for a lesson. He'd be more than pleased."

"Honestly, I'd love that."

The couple admired the koi which followed people around the edges of the pond hoping for a treat. "Greedy aren't they? I think the tourists have spoiled them rotten."

Sadie leaned back in her chair. "The ladies in their kimono move so smoothly. I can fly an aeroplane, but I've never been good at being graceful."

Roger clicked off several photos of the ladies serving tea. "Glad I brought my camera. The kimonos are beautiful. Definitely worth a try to colorize the results. Won't be completely accurate, but I may come close."

He put the camera in his satchel. "And Sadie, you are perfect just the way you are."

Sadie laughed and wiped almond cookie crumbs from her shirtfront. "Glad I have someone bamboozled." She stood and flapped her skirt to let more crumbs fall. "There's a special exhibit at the Lath House. Bonsai plants and a Japanese gardener demonstrating how to grow trees and mosses in miniature landscapes. Something to do with Zen and Buddhism. Sound interesting?"

"Very. I've always been intrigued by bonsais. Remind me of little fairylands. Speaking of the Lath House, I was there two weeks ago with the police. One of the officers spotted a possible tie-in to Dr. Wolf's death in one of my photos."

"Really? The police are still snooping around the place? Is it a clue?"

"Clue? No. Only a coin someone dropped. In any event, there wouldn't be any way to determine who lost it."

Sadie bit into a rice cake. Her second order. "I have a feeling about this, Roger. Asa Wolf might be the story I've been looking for. The big one. The one to make my editor sit up and take notice. He has to see me as a serious reporter, not someone wanting out of the kitchen for an hour or two."

Simon nodded. He loved how passionate Sadie was about her writing.

"Dr. Wolf's life was shadowy, mysterious and ended with a bizarre death. I think my editor and the public would find it fascinating. So tell me. What have the police determined regarding Dr. Wolf's murder?"

"Murder? What murder?"

"Oh don't be coy. It's all over town. A well-known secret, as they say."

He gave her a look which she ignored. "I told you about a coin found in the Lath House. Other than the coin discovery, I can't discuss my work with the police. You know that."

"I do, so I'll just natter on about what I think."

He laughed and ran his fingers through his dark hair. "I wouldn't dare stop you. You always did love a good mystery. And irritatingly, you have the clues sorted out before anyone else. I dare say you could out-Sherlock, Sherlock Holmes."

"Lovely compliment, Roger!" She leaned across the small table. "Okay. First, I absolutely think it *is* murder. One of the Expo gardeners told a *Herald* reporter Wolf was posed as though ready to be put directly into a coffin. People don't drop dead in such a way."

"No argument there."

"I've also been hearing about the good doctor's experimental research on the elusive ailment called female hysteria and his use of electricity. Hopefully, he didn't combine the two. I was told he wanted to be published in a big-time medical journal. Being a big fish in San Diego wasn't good enough. He wanted international fame.

"Others say it was alcohol talking, and he was washed up long ago. But the biggest mystery is: where did all his money come from? The hospital paid well, but not so well he could live the life of a tycoon."

Roger looked surprised. "I can't believe the gossip generated in this town."

Sadie's face was glowing with excitement making Roger want to reach over and plant a kiss on her wonderful lips.

"I'd like to do some snooping around. If I'm right, this might be an award-winning article."

She put her hands in the air like framing a headline. "Sadie Brown: From Weekly Columnist to Investigative Journalist!" Then she burst out with a giggle. "Guess I'm putting the cart before the horse."

"More importantly, you might also be sticking your nose where it's not wanted. You sure you want to put yourself in that kind of position?"

"Oh Roger, don't pooh-pooh my chance to be a journalist. Besides, I already have an appointment tomorrow with Mrs. Wolf."

"She's up for an interview so soon?"

"Strange don't you think? I figured she'd say no but decided to ask. Nothing ventured nothing gained, as Ben Franklin used to say."

"Pretty sure the saying was around long before Franklin was born."

Sadie laughed and slid her hand into Rogers. "Let's go see if we can find a Japanese coin or two before the bonsai lesson. Maybe a few yen escaped the little ones.

* * *

Just as Sadie reached out to ring the doorbell of the Wolf residence, the door swung open.

A well-known sales agent was fastening his briefcase. "I'll be in touch, Mrs. Wolf. Thank you for calling my office."

A young blonde woman dressed in black mourning held the door. "Thank you for coming by so quickly." She held out the man's straw hat for him.

The man saw Sadie and nodded, placed his hat atop his head and walked away.

Lou Wolf smiled and held out her hand to Sadie. "You must be Miss Brown. Please come in. Beth will show you to the terrace while I file away some paperwork in the library. Only take a quick minute. It's lovely on the terrace this morning with the sunshine and all."

Beth, a twenty-something woman, appeared and showed Sadie to the sun-dappled patio area.

"I'll be back with some iced mint water. Please have a seat."

Sadie sat on a patio chair and hoped she looked professional and not as nervous as she felt. For the umpteenth time, she went over the questions she planned to ask. An indelicate query could put an end to the interview before it began. Happily, an iridescent flyer changed her mood in instant. A hummingbird zoomed in to have a close look at the red silk flower on her lapel making Sadie rear back and giggle. Thanks to the daring little bird, her anxiety vanished.

Mrs. Wolf sailed through the doors leading from the library. "Those hummers can be quite bold, but adorable."

She held out her hand to shake. "So nice to meet you, Miss Brown. I've never met a lady reporter before. Please call me Lou, and I'll call you Sadie. Rather silly to be on a last-name basis since you're planning to delve into my husband's research. It makes me extremely happy he and his research are finally going to receive the accolades they deserve. Perhaps there will be a patent or two I can apply for that would bring in a tidy sum. Wouldn't that be nice?"

Sadie was taken aback by Mrs. Wolf's cool, un-widow like manner. Not what Sadie had expected. The anticipated fragile appearance, red eyes and gaunt face from sleepless nights were not in evidence.

"Here comes Beth with the mint-water. I like it mixed with sparkling water. If you prefer, she can bring tea or something stronger."

"Sparkling mint-water is perfect, thank you. Your terrace is beautiful. Such lovely flowers. Won't you miss it?'

Lou set her drink on the table. "Miss it? Oh, you must have recognized the real estate agent. He's an old family friend. He and my father went to the same college. I called him for advice because the house is enormous, and it's built on way too much property. Upkeep is ridiculous. Silly, to have all this for just one person don't you think?"

She smoothed her skirt. "Asa and I never had children. We tried, but something didn't work. We were unhappy about it, but life goes on." She reached for her cigarettes. "May I offer you one? Custom made."

"No thank you, Mrs. Wolf. This is an Irving Gill designed home, isn't it? Shouldn't be difficult to sell."

"Yes, it is a Gill design. And, it cost a pretty penny. But, I plan to sell it...when the time is more seemly...after an appropriate time of grief. Dictates of society and all. However, I believe in doing research early so one is ready for the future. If nothing else, I'm extremely practical."

"True, the dictates of society can be foolish sometimes. You should be able to sell your home whenever you wish without tongues wagging."

Lou smiled. "I'm relieved you agree. Speaking of dictates of society, I applaud your haircut. Is it a must, being a busy newspaper reporter?"

"More for my flying lessons. The leather hat and goggles I have to wear makes long hair difficult."

"Oh, now I'm more impressed. A lady reporter who's learning to fly. But please, you must want to begin with your questions. What can I tell you about my darling, Asa, and his research?"

Sadie opened her notebook. "Let's start with how you met your husband and the type of person he was. A renowned humanitarian I understand."

"Yes. Yes, he was a humanitarian. He went out of his way for all his patients, men and women alike. We met at the San Diego Tennis Club. I was in a tournament, and he was there with my brother. Even though he was old enough to be my father, I fell madly in love on the spot."

Lou stubbed out her cigarette and lit another. "He was the most gentle and loving man I've ever known. He fell for me too but found it difficult to adjust to the age difference." She laughed. "He got over that soon enough. A year later we were married. Although his work came before anything else, he made me feel terribly important. I loved him dearly until the day he died."

Sadie smiled. "It's a love story most women can only dream about. You're most fortunate. What do you know about his education?"

"Asa didn't come from a wealthy family. His parents were teachers who saved and scraped together the funds to send him to college and medical school. He graduated first in his class from USC in Los Angeles. His lifelong interest in research began there.

"Over the years he's done a tremendous amount of research at Agnew. Sadly the hospital and the estate are in a battle over his papers. My attorney says they don't have a leg to stand on. I hope he's right.

"His experiments and such are all over my head. But I have the names of some of his fellow doctors at Agnew who can tell you more about his research."

"Thank you. That would be helpful."

Lou walked inside to write down names and numbers while Beth came to remove the tray of glasses and the empty pitcher. She looked upset, almost angry.

"Excuse me, Beth, do you have something to add to what Mrs. Wolf told me?

"It's not for me to say, Miss."

"I plan to do an in-depth article about Dr. Wolf as a person in addition to his research. Learning about all aspects of his life and personality is important for accuracy. Here's my card. Call me if there's something you want to tell me. I promise whatever you say, your name will never be made public."

Beth pocketed the card. "I don't want to go behind my employer's back, but let's just say Mrs. Wolf did a whitewash job on her husband. He wasn't some kind of saint, not by a long way. That's all I'm going to say."

Driving back to the newsroom, Sadie's intuition told her she'd be hearing from Beth soon.

CHAPTER 12

August 9, 1915

The sun had set, and a chilly breeze whipped off the ocean and swirled around the deserted hilltop Expo grounds. Noted evangelist, Billy Sunday, had preached to an enormous crowd the previous night at the Spreckels Organ Pavilion. His sermon had been particularly vehement about the temptations of what most people called fun and included vivid descriptions of damnation.

Perhaps more as a consequence of Sunday's sermon than the cold weather, the usual evening crowds were nowhere to be found. From one end of the Isthmus fun zone to the other, rides, exhibits, and dancehalls were closing early. Even the Chop Suey Parlor was empty of people except for the Phrenology Study Group.

Dr. Sanders picked at his pork fried rice and looked around the table. Only three other members, all Agnew Sanitarium doctors, had come to the meeting. Club participation was dribbling away since Asa's death. Sanders saw the club was breathing its last. Death had robbed the club of its driving force...Asa and his strong personality.

The daft name, Phrenology Study Group, was only a thin mask to hide their true purpose. Studying bumps and measurements of someone's skull as a way to determine personality was a half-baked pseudoscience. But it was a plausible cover to spend an evening away from nagging wives. Toss in some wine, dancing girls and Asa's premium cigars, it all made a delightful if slightly naughty evening.

"The Isthmus is dead tonight. That Billy Sunday evangelist preached last night at the Organ Pavilion on the temptations of drinking liquor and just having a plain good old time.

"The dancing girls are taking tonight off, I heard. No business they said." Dr. Sanders picked some more at his food. "If I'd known, I'd of stayed home too."

Dr. O'Brien sipped his sake. "Not me. The grandchildren are visiting for a week. A wild bunch of monkeys. Fun for short durations, very short."

"Did some girl reporter try to interview any of you about Asa and his research? She came by my office, but I didn't give her the time of day. Prying into Asa's work won't be good for anyone. She should be home raising a batch of kids at her age."

"I got trapped by her. Dang persistent. She blocked my car, for gosh sakes. I told her Dr. Wolf kept his research to himself, so I couldn't help her with her article. Then she asked about the lawsuit over his papers. How the heck she knew about that is beyond me. A little buttinski is what she is."

Wiping his lips after the last bite of chop suey, Dr. O'Brien cleared his throat. "So what is the latest on the legal battle between Agnew and the Wolf estate? Such a fuss over nothing. As far as I could tell, he stopped writing papers and working on his inventions years ago. He liked to talk a good game that's for sure, especially after a few belts of bourbon. Liked to go on about working on some hush-hush, ground-breaking research and applying for a new patent. All nonsense. Pure nonsense."

"Well however ridiculous his stories, his wife and the hospital believed them. The hospital contends since Asa's work was done within the confines of their building and on their time, they are entitled to the research, etc., etc. I see their point. Something all of us should take note of."

"Someone told me a team of hospital legal eagles is reading through every piece of paper they can find with Wolf's name on it.

After which they'll make a decision to release all, part or none to the estate."

"Legal eagles? What do those rinky-dinks know about medical research? Doubt they'd know a tibia from a fibula. Ridiculous waste of energy and money."

"They won't find anything new. Just his old theories about using electricity for medical treatments. He was a big advocate of combining electric currents with hydroelectric baths to treat hysteria. Never could verify it worked. I heard the patients said they would rather suffer the illness than endure the treatment."

"Wolf was always a big proponent of electrical treatments. 'The most underrated treatment available.' he liked to say. Last I heard, he was rewriting an old paper to present at a conference in San Francisco. 'Electricity and its Place in 20th Century Medicine.'"

"His research. Piffle. So much cock and bull. His drinking however is another story. I'm sorry he's dead, but think it's for the best he won't be performing surgeries any longer. His drinking was becoming a problem."

"Some people can't handle their alcohol. He was one of them. He was the sort Billy Sunday loves to yell and bellow about. And now Sunday's getting people riled up about prohibition."

"Making liquor illegal will never happen, Billy Sunday or no Billy Sunday."

"Maybe. But Carrie Nation and her cohorts are getting people to think liquor is worse than the plague. I wouldn't be surprised to see laws against alcohol happen. And I put the blame on the immigrants. Can't hold their liquor. Going to make it bad for all of us."

O'Brien bristled. "You mean like the Irish?"

"No offense, Patrick. I should clarify. It's the illiterate immigrants. The ones who spend their paycheck in a saloon every Friday night. Can't pay their rent or their kids' doctor bills."

O'Brien nodded and poured more sake in his cup. "I see where you're coming from on that front. But I doubt making liquor illegal will solve the problem."

O'Brien signaled the waiter. "We need more sake. These little bottles don't go far."

"And what about Wolf's private clinic?"

"I'll pretend you didn't mention the place. I had nothing to do with the clinic and will deny any knowledge of it."

Dr. Sanders poured more sake in his cup. "Okay, so much for all that. More to the point, we have to face facts. Our study group is gasping for breath, and just barely alive. I move the Phrenology Study Group be disbanded. Anyone want to second it?"

Dr. O'Brien sighed. "I'll second the motion."

The doctors pulled on their coats, paid the bill and made their way home to their wives, the warmth of a nice fire and good brandy. Thankfully, the O'Brien grandchildren were fast asleep.

* * *

August 10, 1915

Sadie's phone rang. It was Mrs. Wolf's maid, Beth.

"I've been thinking about our talk. I'd like to chat again. There are things I think you should know before you write your article. Tomorrow I have errands to run downtown. Can you meet me someplace out of the way for coffee?"

"Absolutely. How about Fred Harvey's lunchroom at the train station. Sometime in the morning?"

"I can be there at 10:00."

"Good, I'll meet you at ten. And remember your name will be kept confidential. So feel free to share whatever you want."

"I hope so. See you tomorrow."

Sadie wondered how much Beth would share about Dr. Wolf and where it would lead.

* * *

August 11, 1915

10:00 a.m. was perfect for a confidential conversation. The early morning trains had come and gone, and the next train wouldn't be arriving for an hour.

When Sadie entered the almost empty Harvey lunchroom, the enticing smell of freshly brewed coffee and hot cinnamon rolls promised a welcomed cup of coffee and a delicious midmorning snack. Beth gave a little wave from a spot at the large counter. Light from enormous arched windows and an overhead skylight struck her hair giving the impression of an angel waiting to deliver sacred knowledge.

They ordered coffee. A Harvey Girl dressed in her black and white uniform served them and left them to their business.

"I can only stay for a few minutes. I have errands to run for Mrs. Wolf and have to be back to help with lunch."

Sadie took a moment to stir cream and sugar in her coffee and gather her thoughts. "Beth, I appreciate your coming to talk with me about Dr. Wolf. I'm trying to get a feel for what the man was truly like. So tell me what you know. Obviously, you don't agree with Mrs. Wolf's description of her husband. Fairly normal though don't you think? The worst person in the world often becomes a saint to the family after they die. Suddenly people want to think the best of the departed."

Beth blew on her coffee and took a tentative sip. "Lou, Mrs. Wolf that is, is well aware her husband isn't a saint. He had a long list of lady friends, mostly nurses, but not exclusively. He'd go after just about anyone who wore a skirt. He seemed compelled to try to seduce women on general principles. A cad through and through. Even worse after a few drinks."

"Did he ever try to seduce you?"

"Of course. I wear a skirt, don't I? I made it clear I had no interest, and he gave up after a few tries, mostly anyway. Heading up the surgery department at Agnew may have had something to do with his skirt-chasing. Men in powerful positions are like that, they get to thinking they're allowed to do whatever they please...don't you think?"

"No. Well not always. Sometimes. There are some men in power who expect all females to find them irresistible. The bad apples. We forget the good men in authority. And to be fair, there are women who find power and money seductive."

"True enough. And to be honest, Lou would be considered that type of women. She was always more interested in money than a love match. Played her romances and her marriage like a game. She always went for the older men with money. Made them feel a little insecure now and then over the age difference and snuck in a bit of flirting with other men. Not too much. She was smart and kept flirting to a minimum. Just enough to keep them on their toes.

"Of course, she had no plans to leave Wolf. Too much money would be left on the table if there was a split. I warned her more than once she was walking a fine line. Her games could turn dangerous."

The conversation took a sharp turn. "What I can't understand is the police or the coroner or whoever not signing off on the death certificate. Do you know anything about that? I mean, he died of a heart attack, didn't he? I know the man made a lot of enemies, especially at the hospital. But good grief, I don't think anyone would want to murder him for being a bully and stabbing people in the back and stuff." Beth dabbed a spot of coffee on the counter with her napkin.

"And the insurance company is being downright silly. Not a dime in payout until whoever signs the certificate...official-like."

"Insurance? Not something I'm looking into, but I'd guess there would be a generous payout. You know how insurance companies can seem to drag their feet when there's big money involved."

"I don't know the exact amount, but yes it would be a lot. Only the best for Dr. Wolf, including insurance benefits bigger than anyone else's. If murder is involved, you don't think Lou would be a suspect, do you? I mean it couldn't have been her. All those doctors he worked with and the ex-mistresses would have more reason than Lou."

Beth looked down at the remains of her half-finished coffee. "I think I've said enough. I'd better get going. Mrs. Wolf's driver is waiting for me. I need to finish my errands and go back to help the cook. Nice woman but thinks she's special...learned to cook in San Francisco at some fancy restaurant, Le Coq or some such. Orders me around something fierce! But, guess I should be grateful I have a job. I've been with Mrs. Wolf for a long time, but..." She shrugged.

Sadie had questions about Wolf's income but thought Beth wouldn't be aware of the Wolfs' financial situation.

"I'll get the bill, Beth. Thank you again. You've been most helpful." Sadie watched Beth walk out of the restaurant. Beth's concern about Wolf's death certificate and the insurance money seemed out of place. But maybe she was concerned about having a job if the money dried up.

She watched a large sedan pull up for Beth. The driver opened the door for her and helped her inside. It was heartening to see. With women fighting for the vote and equality, the cause might lead to the loss of some social niceties such as opening a woman's door or helping a gal on with her coat. She hoped not. Regardless, the vote and equality should be for everyone. At least California had seen the light. Women in the state had gained the right to vote in 1911.

The Harvey girl refilled her coffee while Sadie made notes regarding her conversation with Beth. Interesting that Beth's information was less about Wolf and more about the death certificate, the insurance policy, and the possibility Wolf was murdered.

Was Beth worried about losing her job? Or did Mrs. Wolf send Beth with a story to divert suspicion away from the widow as a killer? Unfortunately, Beth had made Lou Wolf sound like a prime suspect. But Mrs. Wolf was just one in a long line of people wishing Dr. Asa Wolf dead.

Nevertheless, Wolf seems to have been a complete cad. It was time to dig deeper into where his money was coming from and into his research...the research the sanitarium was so intent on keeping away from the hands of the doctor's estate. Was it because the research could lead to money producing patents or perhaps something the hospital wished to keep hidden?

More than one sanitarium had been closed due to unethical practices seeing the light of day. Highly unlikely in Agnew's case but one did have to wonder what the hospital's legal team was looking for.

Most of the doctors on Lou's list had already refused Sadie's requests for an interview. Another avenue would be the nurses. They might be more forthcoming.

She felt disappointed with people stonewalling her. Finding accurate and truthful information was like fighting her way through a swamp. Not that it would stop her sleuthing. She was on a quest and fully expected to reach her goal: discover the identity of the killer and write a newspaper that would keep people talking for weeks.

.

CHAPTER 13

Aug 16, 1915

Mrs. Wolf's brother sat in his hospital office staring out the window. The view was magnificent, but Fayette Watkins had long ago stopped admiring it. He marveled at how quickly he had taken the view and his position at the hospital for granted.

Should have counted his blessing because he might lose this office and his job. His position at the hospital was on shaky grounds with Asa dead and buried. He wasn't stupid. He knew he had gained his position due to Asa's recommendation. His education was not up to snuff, and there were a couple of exaggerations on his resume that wouldn't hold up under close scrutiny.

Earlier, a clerk had alerted him his personnel file had been ordered up by a newly founded hospital review board. The information had left him with a sick feeling.

He turned back to his desk, his mail, and the morning paper. As usual, the front page was full of the war raging in Europe. Sharing page one was a photograph and an article about aviator, Art Smith's heart-stopping loop-the-loop over the Expo grounds. The newspaper prattled on about the man and his amazing flying skills. Waste of good newsprint in Watkins opinion. He thought the flying fad would soon die away. The sooner the better actually.

After all, what use was it? He couldn't foresee any benefit from such a circus show.

"Sir?" A clerk appeared at his office door. "The Review Board would like to know if you are available for a brief meeting."

Fayette adjusted his tie. "When? I'll check my calendar."

"Now, sir. Unless you have a patient waiting."

"I can be there in ten minutes. I need to finish up some notes from my last examination."

"Yes, sir. I'll tell them." The clerk gave him a worried look and left.

Fayette felt ill. As always, he expected the worse. He could quite possibly be looking for a new position without a letter of recommendation before the day was done.

Thankfully he had no wife or children who expected a large house and the finer things in life. He did have a stash of gold and some unset diamonds hidden at home, but it was emergency money. It would barely cover him for three months. Then there would be nothing left for food or rent. He'd be out on the street with no job. The Paal painting would bring a tidy sum, but his parents would never forgive him if he sold what was considered a family heirloom brought from the old country.

The thoughts floating through Dr. Watkins head made him sweat. He stood and made his way to the hospital's conference room.

Five grim-faced men stood (accept a wheelchair-bound war veteran) and offered him a chair. "Please Dr. Watkins, take a seat. We've been asked to look over some personnel files for possible replacements for Dr. Wolf's position."

Fayette's eyes were glued to a stack of files placed prominently on the table. The man continued, "Just getting started. However, we stopped due to a strange turn of events."

Fayette looked at the board members. None were smiling, although a few watched his face closely.

"Sadly, we've found several problems and improprieties."

'So, this is how it ends.' thought Fayette. 'My position, my reputation, my career...all gone in the next few minutes.'

"To be honest, we are rather shocked. But these incidents do happen where men and women work together. We are very disappointed though when one considers the upstanding reputation of our doctors and surgeons."

Fayette looked around the table. "Men and women working together? I don't understand."

"Dr. Watkins, you worked closely with Dr. Wolf. In addition, you're related to him by marriage."

"Yes. That's true. But I don't understand why you asked to meet with me."

"Yes. Well. To be blunt, there appears to have been an unfortunate association between Dr. Wolf and a nurse here at the hospital by the name of Rose Trigby."

Feeling like a fish who just freed itself from a fisherman's hook, Fayette's sense of relief was overwhelming.

"We assume Dr. Wolf kept this wretched affair from you since his wife is your sister. However, in the pursuit of obtaining all pertinent information, we feel a duty to ask if you knew of the situation?"

"No, no I did not. Asa had his foibles, as great men often do, but this was one foible I wasn't aware of. I hope the details of this can be kept from my sister. She's in a fragile state, as you can imagine."

"Yes, of course. You have our word on that. This is an extremely awkward situation brought to our attention by a letter from someone who no longer works for the hospital."

Fayette looked around the table. "While I realize this is all quite upsetting, I want to say Nurse Trigby is an outstanding nurse. I hope she'll be able to keep her position here. She'll be terribly difficult to replace. Such experienced nurses are hard to find."

"We have yet to decide. We want to gather all the facts and discuss the issue. It could be a tempest in a teapot for all we know, something fabricated and completely untrue."

One of the Board members held up a folder. "Just so you know Dr. Watkins. You are on our list of possible candidates for the vacant position." He and the others smiled.

Fayette crept back to his office hoping to collapse in his chair before his knees gave out.

* * *

Roger was putting away equipment in his photography studio after a society shoot. A socially prominent matron had called for an appointment to photograph her daughter and fiancé. An engagement photograph was needed. Today, if at all possible. It's an emergency the matron said. An engagement announcement was set to run in the Sunday papers.

The emergency was obvious when the couple arrived. The bride-to-be glowed and kept a protective hand on her stomach. The soon-to-be groom's appearance was haggard from an apparent late night of drinking. The man was green around the gills. Roger was grateful the groom managed to keep from vomiting, although he kept a trash bin at the ready. There were times it was touch and go.

Roger kept the photoshoot short, and the matron and delighted bride-to-be left to make wedding plans. The groom could be described as beyond grateful to be released from the ordeal...most likely to go home and pass out for the rest of the day.

Relieved everyone had gone, Roger opened the windows wide. He hoped the miserable, dismal mood left by the potential groom would be blown out to sea. Thankfully it didn't take long for the scent of the roses from the garden to sweep through the room. Roger could almost feel the gloom flee out the window, race past the gardens, and down the hill to the ocean.

The summer wedding engagement backdrops were stored away just as Buckley arrived with an announcement. "Sergeant Greenway from the San Diego Police is here to see you."

"Sergeant Greenway, pleasure to see you. Please come in. May I offer you some of Buckley's freshly brewed iced tea or maybe something more potent? Is this an official visit or...?"

"Official. Only here for a brief minute to ask a favor."

"Okay. How can I help?"

"Thanks to Miss Brown's gossipy friend, we did some checking and came up with the names of two women we think Dr. Wolf forced from their jobs. Both were living and working fulltime in Northern California at the time of the murder.

"We also learned of a nurse who left town unannounced and was never heard from again. A sister in Ohio reported her missing. Because of our investigations, I have no doubt there are other women. And who knows, maybe patients too. The man was a complete rogue."

"So it seems."

"Men like him let a little power go to their heads. He needed to be taken down a notch or two. Can't prove it, but I'm guessing someone was angry enough to do just that."

Greenway walked to the open window and watched a ferry make its way across the bay to Coronado. "Great view, Roger." He turned back and gathered his thoughts.

"The department wants to close the books on its 'official' investigation of Wolf's death. Nothing new has turned up. It's been like pulling porcupine quills from a dog's nose to get information. Dr. Wolf's associates and the hospital claim Wolf could be brusk but was an exceptional surgeon and admired by all. No enemies, no unhappy patients, etc., etc. Everyone, including Mrs. Wolf, would lead us to believe he was some version of Saint Cyrus the Physician."

"Saint who?"

"Forgive me. My dear Catholic mother had me memorizing saints at a young age, even before I learned the rules of stickball.

"My superior wants me working on a cargo theft case at the docks and Henderson back making sure downtown businesses are behaving themselves. But I'm fighting it. Frankly, my temperament won't let me give up. I can't let Wolf's killer get away with murder. It's stuck in my craw.

"What this is all leading up to...I'm here to ask for a favor."

"Okay. What's the favor?"

"It's about Miss Brown. Do you think she would poke around and ask a few questions for me...in her capacity as a reporter? It would be most helpful if she would inquire about Wolf's research, where his money came from, people he angered. Not to push things mind you. I don't want to put her in any danger. However, working for the *Herald* is the perfect cover. But (and this is a big but), I don't want anyone at the SDPD to know about it. I'm breaking some rules here." He grimaced. "Guess you could say, I'm desperate."

Roger laughed. "Well, this will make her day. To be honest, she's already snooping into Wolf and his death. She thinks an article about his research on female hysteria and his strange death could be her ticket to moving up from a weekly columnist to a full-fledged investigative reporter.

"She's one of those people who love a good mystery. Besides, she has concluded, quite on her own, he was murdered. And, importantly, she can be relentless."

"Sounds like a perfect fit. Again, I hope I'm making myself clear. This would be strictly between the three of us. A reporter getting involved with a police investigation is heavily discouraged. I'd be first in line to tell a reporter to mind his own business. But I think in this instance, Sadie is perfect to help our investigation."

"She'll be delighted to hear it, Sgt. Greenway."

Roger looked out at his garden. "Dr. Cohen mentioned the angel trumpet plant at the Lath House. Did he find anything in the organ or blood specimens he kept from Wolf?"

"No. But according to a local botanist, there's a goldmine of poisonous plants on the Expo grounds and in private gardens all over San Diego. Some will trigger a heart attack. If Jules turns up proof of a poison, I will be doubly interested in investigating Wolf's nurses...and his wife. The public finds it difficult to believe a woman is capable of murder. But it does happen, and more often than people would like to believe. And women are far more likely to use poison than men."

"What about all the men he used as stepping stones to get to his position at the hospital?"

"Wolf did make enemies among his co-workers. Enough to kill? Maybe. There are other possibilities besides co-workers. I'm making the rounds to question his book collecting friends, wine appreciation groups, and a men's club he belonged to."

"You're dedicated."

"You could say that. Although, I think dedicated is a nice way of saying I'm fixated." Evan laughed. "Also, I wanted to tell you, a friend of yours came by the station looking for a book Wolf supposedly had on his person. Simon, he said his name was."

"Good grief. If it was Simon Bennet, he's no friend of mine. He introduced himself to me at a charity event weeks back asking if I had seen a book at the Lath House. Strange man and certainly no friend."

"Happy to hear that. He struck me as a smooth talker up to no good. His trip to the station and his questions made me suspicious. I'll be checking into his connection to Wolf, no doubt about it."

"Good idea. My thoughts exactly."

"So, you'll ask Sadie to do a bit of spying for us? In a covert way?"

"Yes. In fact, I look forward to it. The thought of being some sort of undercover police informant will thrill her to no end."

"Thanks. The article she wants to write is a perfect cover. But tell her to be careful and stay absolutely quiet about helping the police. And never suggest in any way she might know who the killer is. It's a surefire way to put herself in danger. I'd never forgive myself if she provoked the murderer."

* * *

Sadie leaned back in Roger's dark brown leather sofa with a sigh. "Perfect night isn't it? Nice dinner, good wine and a splendid murder mystery to read."

"And the perfect companion by your side."

"Well, that goes without saying."

"I have some news you'll like."

"Really? What?"

"Sergeant Greenway came by today to ask if you would ask around, discreetly of course, regarding Dr. Wolf and pass anything interesting on to him. Any information you learn would be for him alone. No one else in the Department is to know."

"Kind of like a police informant? Undercover work but just for Greenway?"

"Exactly like a police informant. A very, very cautious informant."

"Okay." She opened her book.

"Okay? Just okay? I thought you'd be thrilled."

She leaned over and kissed him on the cheek. "That's been my plan all along. The article I'm writing is terribly important, but I planned to pass on anything that could lead to the murderer directly to Greenway. It's the right thing to do."

"Right. But do be careful, please." Roger picked up his new photography book. "If I didn't say thank you for the book before, let me say so now. Great book full of good advice."

"Glad you like it. My book is lovely too. Can't get enough of the Father Brown series."

"Sadie?"

"Yes?"

"You will be careful, won't you?"

"Aren't I always? Don't worry. I plan to be careful."

"Promise?"

"Cross my heart." She leaned across and gave him another kiss.

Roger looked at the gal that made his heart glow and wished he wouldn't worry, but he would.

CHAPTER 14

Aug 28, 1915

The AT&SF Railroad's new Baldwin engine erupted steam and roared through the summer countryside of Southern California. The engine pulled a long line of passenger cars. Inside, the passengers who bothered to glance out the windows observed brown, sun-scorched rolling hills. When the train thundered towards the coastline, the dry grasses changed to yellow-green. Relentless foggy mornings along the ocean kept the grass green through most of June and July. But it was late August, and the grass was giving up the fight.

Roger looked out the train's window and watched the ocean sparkling in the sun. He had tried to read a book but eventually gave up. Travel by train was always a disappointment and an uncomfortable experience for Roger. He found it noisy, jarring and the "cushioned" seats had been used far too long by a family of elephants.

The 55-mile trip from San Diego to Fallbrook for their Olive Day celebration was manageable, but 220-miles to Barbara was bottom numbing.

He was reminded anew he should have gone by boat. Steamers were far more comfortable, and he found travel on the ocean refreshing. Too late now. The trip was almost over, and a week in beautiful Santa Barbara lay ahead.

The picturesque city with its seaside setting and gentle hills was a mecca for artists. Taking advantage of their location, each year Santa Barbara hosted a three-day artist's symposium. Photography had been included as part of the curriculum this year. "Color Tinting Prints" and "Ocean Photographs That Win Awards" were at the top of his must-attend list. Three full days of photography lectures and classes were ahead. And someone from Alfred Stieglitz' studio was a keynote speaker. He couldn't be happier.

He had just re-read the schedule of classes when he spied Simon Bennet smoking a cigarette on the outside platform between cars. Having no desire to be recognized by the man, he turned his back and looked out the window for the last remaining miles.

At the train station, an old school friend was waiting. Eddie, a classically trained pianist, worked for the silent film company, Flying A Studios. When the film company was located in La Mesa, just east of San Diego, Eddie began playing mood music (happy, sad, romantic, etc.) for the actors during filming. After a year in La Mesa, Flying A packed up and moved to greener pastures...Santa Barbara. Eddie moved too. Roger missed their friendship.

Eddie grabbed Roger in a bear hug. "Wow! So great to see you, Roger."

"You too Eddie. So, what do you think of your new town? Looks beautiful."

"It is. It is, and the location is perfect for making movies. We're churning out two-reelers like you couldn't believe. La Mesa was nice, but Santa Barbara is better by a mile. With the studio making endless westerns, there's no better location to film. Plus, the ocean is perfect for romance and pirate movies. If that's not enough we're closer to Hollywood than we were in La Mesa. Perfect if we need equipment or spare parts."

Roger laughed. "Sounds like Nirvana." It was terrific to see his friend so excited and animated.

"You bet it is. I forgot to mention when I wrote you, but I hope you brought your swim togs. Jimmie & I are having a pool party at our place tomorrow. The place will be jumping with gorgeous women and lots of food and booze and…hey, are you listening?"

"Oh sorry, buddy. I see a guy over there I'd like to avoid. Didn't realize he was going to get off here. Let's get on to your place if that's okay."

"No problem. Here give me a bag. Almost forgot, I know this guy, Morrie. He's a genius when it comes to camera angles and lighting. He's the studio's lead camera guy. I can arrange a meetup with him if you'd like."

"That's great! Didn't expect that, but I'd appreciate it. I'll be at the conference Monday through Wednesday. Ask him if Thursday or Friday would work with his schedule."

Eddie's yellow 1914 Trumbull roadster cyclecar was parked next to the station and was soon loaded with luggage and camera gear. There was barely room for the two men, but they managed to squeeze in and were off.

At Eddie and roommate Jimmie's Spanish style bungalow, Roger was able to catch up with Eddie's current life and mutual friends.

"Hey remember Seymour from La Mesa Music School? He said to tell you 'Hi.' He's playing piano at a movie studio in Hollywood. The pay is great, hard to resist."

"Redheaded Seymour? I thought he'd be playing concerts or working for a symphony. Obviously, the money is in the film studios. You still enjoy playing mood music for a bunch of actors? What'd you call them? Brainless pretty boys?"

"Yep. Most of them would rather listen to Al Jolson than Mozart, but I still love the job. And I get to watch my roommate, Jimmie, do his stuff. He's brilliant. Should be on stage. He doesn't know it, but the studio pays me extra to make sure he doesn't get overly cozy with the booze. His contract is only good if he stays sober on set. But watch out on the weekends. Well, you'll see tomorrow at the pool party. Now tell me how things are going with you and your sassy girlfriend. You are one lucky man finding someone like her."

Party day was warm and sunny…perfect for a pool party. The patio was made for partying. Every bare spot had been paved with vibrant Mexican tiles. Ivy climbed the sides of the house and the fences, and red hibiscus bushes ran riot in the garden.

Guests arrived early in their most colorful getups. So much color, Roger wished he had learned to paint. Booze, a spread of good food, splashing in the pool and gossiping about the studio kept everyone entertained. With all the screaming and laughing, Roger expected the police to come calling. But the neighbors either didn't mind or gave up long ago.

"Eddie is Jimmie okay? He seems a little under the weather."

"Last night he started on a bottle of Jack Daniels as soon as he walked in the front door. Now he's hungover. No worry, he'll be pouring himself a drink and diving in the pool before you know it."

Jimmie didn't get crazy, but he drank more than was good for him. Roger saw a rocky road ahead for the fresh-faced actor. A talented young man surrounded by people who wouldn't or couldn't say no to his unhealthy lifestyle didn't bode well.

Although Morrie, the lead cameraman had taken a pass on the party to attend a baseball game with his sons, he sent his regards and a time to meet at the studio Thursday morning. Besides, there were other studio people at the party who were happy to offer filming tips and tricks.

* * *

After three days of classes and demonstrations, Roger rode with Eddie to work at the studio. It was a kick to watch Eddie play the piano to set the right mood for the actors. But when the time came to film a melodramatic death scene, Roger couldn't contain his laugh. When the director glared in his direction, Roger stepped outside to compose himself. Eddie was soon beside him.

"They're changing the set, so I get a break for thirty minutes. Let's walk over to Morrie's set. Did I tell you American is the largest film studio in the world, and the best I might add?"

"Eddie, my friend, you've found your niche. Can't remember the last time I saw you so happy."

Morrie was a generous man who enjoyed showing Roger how things operated at the studio. He was more than happy to discuss the cameras and lighting equipment in detail. Roger listened, watched, and soaked it all in. The trip up the coast was worth it for Morrie's expert guidance alone.

"Join me for lunch at the VIP lunchroom? One of the perks for being in charge of the camera and lighting. Do you like crab? The crab salad is a specialty."

They ordered and were sharing stories about Kodak when Roger saw Simon enter the room. He was in the company of a tall gray-haired man wearing plaid slacks and a red sweater. The two were animatedly discussing something and paid no attention to the other people in the VIP Room.

"Morrie, do you know the man in the red sweater?"

"He's our art director, also known as 'The Professor.' Think he's Greek. Talented guy, but glad I don't have to deal with him and his fractured English. He finds or makes most of the film sets and the props. I'm always amazed at what he finds or creates out of thin air in a place like Santa Barbara. Too bad he can't produce cameras or lights. Our biggest problem in Santa Barbara is its lack of resources when equipment needs fixing or replacing. Fortunately, Los Angeles is only 80 some miles down the coast, and they have just about anything.

"Los Angeles isn't Chicago or New York but it's growing, especially the movie trade. That greedy, sue-happy Thomas Edison and his camera patents are forcing the film industry to California. Not that California is the worst place to work. But Edison and his thugs are making filmmakers miserable unless they pay him huge bucks."

"I hadn't heard that."

"Yeah. Some men get a little money and it goes to their heads."

* * *

Simon Bennet added a handful of oyster crackers to his clam chowder and half a shaker of pepper. The conversation with The Professor was not going well.

"We have searched every place we can think of. Asa's death has put us in a real bind. The museum in New York wants to see the logbook and the map so their experts can take a look at it. How long before you can duplicate the book and the treasure map?"

The Professor took a bite of his sandwich and scowled. He had a heavy accent but made himself clear about creating a second set. "Sorry, Mr. Bennet. It's your problem, not mine the logbook and map they are missing. I am too busy. My work here is at full maximum. You tell your buyer, the name I do not want to know, the log is gone."

Simon felt desperate and maybe a little sweaty even, but pressed on. "The rainy season is coming. Doesn't the rain slow down movie production? Would you be able to create another log and map then?"

"Yes. Sometimes yes. Maybe the holidays and rainy season coming up. I have your phone number. I call you in November or maybe not...if it suits my timepiece...timetable."

"Same price?"

"Yes - $1,500. Like last time. If I do it."

Simon kept his face poker still. Fury! He was filled with it. He wanted to rip someone's arms off! Someone by the name of Asa Wolf! Good thing the SOB was six-feet under and he couldn't get at him. That damnable bastard had collected $1,000 each from him, Ezra and Jeffry. Asa had said in all seriousness, "If we each pitch in $1,000, that'll cover the $4,000 fee the Professor wants for his work. A little pricey, but well worth it."

Tamping down his anger, Simon submitted. "Right then. I'll expect a call in November. In the meantime, I'll stall our buyer."

He left the VIP Room so livid about Asa's double-con he noticed no one including Roger who sat three tables away with the lead cameraman.

CHAPTER 15

Sept 10, 1915

September 10, 1915, burst into San Diego sunny, bright, and warm. It was Movie Day at the Expo. The hospital's female staff (and a few men) were all atwitter. Famous silent film actor, Francis X. Bushman would be at the Expo for the entire day and into the evening. The Exposition had planned a spectacular dinner and ball to honor him and actress, Beverly Bayne. However, the staff didn't give a hoot about Miss Bayne, only handsome, sexy Mr. Bushman.

Finishing their breakfast shift in the kitchen, six female food preparers gossiped about rumors surrounding Bushman and frequent co-star, Beverly Bayne.

"Poor Mrs. Bushman. Married thirteen years to such a gorgeous man and birthed five of his children, and this is the thanks she gets."

"He wouldn't cheat on his wife. I don't believe it for a moment!"

"I heard he's an honest, God-fearing Christian. He'd never do something so dishonorable."

"Maybe it's all a bunch of publicity gossip."

Gladys, the chief salad maker patted her newly coiffed hair. "Bought me a new hat from the Sears Roebuck catalog awhile back. Perfect for today. Purple and red ostrich feathers it has. I'll be turning a head or two. One of them might even be Mr. Bushman's his self."

"Turning heads? You'll be a full-on spectacle is more like it, I'd say, Gladys."

The kitchen crew all laughed good-naturedly including Gladys.

"Lunch crew should be here soon. I'll meet you all at the trolley stop in front of the Expo's front gate?"

"Right. Can't wait to get a look at his self and Miss Bayne together."

"They're actors. Won't show nothing I expect."

"True. But I don't care one way or the other, just want to stare at the man and do some daydreaming."

"I'm gonna try for an autograph. Oh, my heart is fluttering already."

Following the last comment, the doors flew open and the dishwashing boys arrived ready to start the breakfast wash-up. The ladies donned their summer coats and hats and sounding like a gaggle of excited seagulls left to ready themselves for Movie Day at the Expo.

* * *

Aloof from the excitement, Rose stared out from a third-floor window at the street below watching the early morning traffic. It was always a take-your-life-in-your-hands jumble between horse-drawn wagons and carriages, automobiles and pedestrians.

She had worked a midnight shift. It was not a shift she cared for. As soon as she finished her patient log, she could go home. There was a lot on her agenda for today.

First on her schedule was a locksmith. He had promised to be waiting for her when she arrived at her apartment. With any luck he wouldn't take too long, she had plans to go to Marston Department store for their end-of-summer hat sale. After which, she had a grocery list that needed attention. Then if she could, she'd squeeze in a nap before her dinner date.

* * *

"You did what?"

Sadie placed the phone earpiece back into its hook. "I made an appointment for you with Dr. Watkins at the sanitarium. Lucky us, he had a cancellation. We can go right over. While you're talking with him, I'll nose around and see what kind of nurse gossip I can pick up."

"You're treading on dangerous ground you know, so please be cautious."

"I promise to be careful, extra careful in fact."

There were many reasons Roger adored Sadie. After honesty and intelligence, her zest and determination attracted him most. But it caused worry at the same time. "So back to the appointment. What kind of problem am I supposed to discuss with Watkins?"

"Your leg for starters. Maybe he's read or heard about new developments in the treatment of post-polio problems such as your leg spasms."

"I think Watkins specializes in TB patients."

"Okay, tell him you have a cough. Whatever. Just keep asking questions for fifteen or twenty minutes. And while you're there, ask about the Bayer pain pills you take. I have serious concerns about those pills for your leg spasms."

"Bayer Laboratories is an excellent and highly thought of Drug Company. And I can find the pills at any drugstore. Heroin is not a big deal. I promise."

She stared at him and scrunched up her lips.

"Okay, I'll ask. You're such a worrywart sometimes."

"And don't forget a warm coat. It's chilly out today."

Sadie had become tired of riding in the motorcycle's sidecar since the weather turned cooler. But she hoped Roger would figure out it was time to start using his automobile on his own. Sounding like a pushy girlfriend was the last thing she wanted. But sometimes men needed a nudge or two.

* * *

The weather had turned even colder by the time they left Dr. Watkins office. Roger and Sadie had lunch at Fred Harvey's Lunchroom at the train station to compare notes and warm up.

"Before you ask, Dr. Watkins said the pills I'm taking are perfectly fine. As long as heroin, like morphine, is taken moderately and only for pain, there should be no problem. Anyway, it may be a moot point. He says Bayer and some other European drug makers plan to stop importing their pills because of a tax bill passed last year. He gave me a prescription for a different pill from a local supplier. Think they're morphine. So that was question number one.

"Number two question: he knows of no new treatment for post-infantile paralysis. He said I'm lucky I had finished growing when I caught polio. It left me with weak muscles in my bad leg, but it's only a fraction shorter than the good leg. My limp is barely noticeable and only when I'm tired and overdo things. Everything he told me, I already knew. Number three: My lungs are perfect."

Sadie sighed. "I don't know if I agree with Dr. Watkins' assessment about heroin and morphine, but it's difficult to argue with an expert."

"Hope you have some news for Sergeant Greenway, because paying for a doctor bill as cover for your investigation means we are having sandwiches instead of steak for lunch."

Sadie laughed. "I love Harvey's hot turkey sandwich with mashed potatoes and gravy. Don't know what they do but their turkey gravy is so much better than mine. My mouth is watering already."

"Perfect place then. So let's hear your report."

"Plenty of gossip. Maybe some of it is on the mark. I took a magazine and stood around the corner from the nurses' desk. The ladies are more than a little upset, and I heard plenty. The entire hospital staff is walking on eggshells. A review team is checking into to Dr. Wolf's rumored escapades. Heads are going to roll if the review team finds employees knew Wolf forced nurses to quit and didn't report it. The nurses think it's all about money. Seems the hospital board is mostly financial people, and the cost of hiring new help and getting them trained is expensive."

She savored a bite of the turkey sandwich and gravy. "The ladies talked about four women who quit without giving notice and left town over the past five years. Appears one now works in Stockton and the other in Napa. Then they talked about a nurse by the name of Rose Trigby. Guess she was Wolf's latest lady love. Sounded like she's still working at the hospital."

"That's interesting. While I was in his office, Dr. Watkins took a call. He said, 'That's perfect. I'll see you tonight. Bye, Rose.' Maybe Rose Trigby? Do you think she would hook up with another man so soon? Wolf is barely in his grave."

"I don't see why not if she was just going along to get along. It's possible she didn't care for Wolf and was just thinking about getting ahead at her job. Only Rose Trigby knows the answer to that. Also heard the nurses say Watkins is in line for Wolf's job as head of surgery at the hospital. So, if Rose is bed-hopping to get ahead, she's moving in the right direction.

"And the nurses made a pact not to acknowledge anything to the review board. They plan to plead ignorance if asked about Wolf and his nurses. The women need their jobs, especially the single ones. With the price of food and rent these days, I completely understand."

Sadie took the last bite of her mashed potatoes and set her fork down. The Harvey Girl refilled her coffee.

"Something just occurred to me. A fox coat was dropped in the Salvation Army's collection box sometime after Asa Wolf died. Fur coats are a difficult sell for a charity shop. They don't want to give it away, but a fair asking price is a month's wage for some. The coat has been making the rounds of the charity stores, La Mesa, Encinitas, even all the way to Oceanside."

Roger finished his coffee wondering where the story was going.

"Last week it was sent to the charity store where I help out. Someone said it's going to go to a Hollywood thrift store if we can't sell it. One of the gals at the store told me the coat has a label in an inside pocket with the owner's name. I think she told me the label said, 'To Rose something-or-other / From some initials I can't recall.' I'll check it next time I help out at the shop."

Sadie gulped down her coffee and turned to Roger. "On second thought, let's go as soon as we're finished here."

"Good idea. It could be an important piece of information Sergeant Greenway would like to have."

* * *

The noise of the Harley made further conversation impossible. Arriving outside the charity shop they saw the silver fox fur displayed prominently in the window surrounded by plain but serviceable winter coats.

Removing her hat and running her fingers through her hair, Sadie decided being pushy was far better than ten days of coughing and blowing her nose with a chest cold. She was past the nudging stage.

"Roger, I think it's time you put your motorcycle away for the summer and bring out the town car. We're both going to catch our death."

Roger laughed. "Really Sadie. Wifely nagging? First making a doctor's appointment for me and now suggesting I bring the Pierce Arrow out of storage because of the change of seasons? Think we'd better start looking for engagement rings."

Sadie was taken aback and then giggled. Pulling her wool coat close she said, "If that's an honest-to-goodness marriage proposal, my answer is 'Yes.'"

"You don't mind I didn't get down on one knee? I was planning a proper proposal with a ring, roses, and Champagne, but what I said kind of slipped out. I do mean it though, in all honesty. And just to be clear, you did say 'Yes', right?"

"Of course, I said 'Yes,' you silly goose. Now let's go take a look at the coat. We can discuss rings after we do our sleuthing business."

Roger grinned. "It's a red-letter day all around."

Inside the store was quiet and empty of customers. With a lack of buyers rummaging through the aisles, the volunteers were folding, hanging clothing and arranging knickknacks on shelves. The shop had a never-ending supply of donations.

One of the shop volunteers looked up as the bell above the door rang out. "Hey, kiddo. What ya doing here today?"

"Just looking around. Girls this is my friend, Roger Siebert. The Roger I'm always talking about?"

The volunteer smirked. "Oh yeah, your 'friend' friend. The one who collects postcards. Pleased to meet ya. You're one of them fancy picture takers, ain't ya?"

Roger laughed good-naturedly. "I am a picture taker, but wouldn't call myself 'fancy.'"

"I'm going to show him some of the cards that just came in."

Roger looked at the postcards and then made his way around the shop. He stopped at the manikin wearing the fur, checked out the inside pocket, removed the coat from the wooden model, and took it to the checkout desk.

"No postcards today, but I will purchase this coat."

"A posh guy like you buying a fur coat at a charity shop? Don't that beat all? Heard everything now."

Roger smiled. "I'm all for a good buy."

As they left, Sadie said. "Bet we'd get an earful if we were inside right now. Jennie doesn't know what 'check your thoughts before you speak' means. But she's never mean spirited. She and the other gals are good eggs.

"So, what did you see in the pocket?"

"There's a label that says: 'Rose T from AW.' Think Sergeant Greenway needs to see this. Would you like me to take you home where it's warm before I stop by the police station?"

"Not on your life. I want the satisfaction of meeting Sergeant Greenway firsthand and hearing what he has to say."

At the same moment, aviatrix, Katherine Stinson was flying a loop-the-loop over San Diego and dropping flowers on the onlookers below. Both Katherine Stinson and Sadie Brown felt high as kites with satisfaction

CHAPTER 16

September 10, 1915

Riding home, Rose couldn't shake the feeling someone in the trolley was watching her. Keeping her head down, she peeked from the corners of her eyes, but no one was paying her any attention. It was guilt and fear, pure and simple. Both would eat her alive if she didn't stop thinking about what happened to Asa and about her job at the hospital. The damnable Review Board was going to find out about the two of them. She knew it deep down in the pit of her being. Would she have a job left? And what would the police think if the board told them?

She walked to her apartment building putting one foot in front of the other as calmly as possible. The locksmith wasn't waiting, so she searched the apartment on her own. No signs of an unwanted visitor. Her flat was as she left it.

The locksmith arrived at Noon with apologies for being late. She showed him the two doors needing new locks. "The front door of course, but also the kitchen door leading onto the drying porch."

The locksmith nodded. "I'd also suggest a new lock on the door leading from your drying porch to the back stairs."

"But it's all screening. Anyone could cut through the screen, reach in, and unlock the door if they wanted in."

He held up a hand. "I know, anyone could get to the lock. But, I can add a piece of plywood on both sides of the door. After I finish with it, a person would have to fly to get to the screening to cut it and get in. Even on the second floor, a woman living alone can't be too cautious these days. What do you think?"

Before she could answer, someone knocked at the opened front door.

"Hello? Miss Trigby? It's the police, ma'am."

Officer Bart Henderson was standing in the doorway smoothing his handlebar mustache, and looking around the living room.

"Miss Trigby?" He didn't bother introducing himself. He was dressed in uniform after all. And he was a little perturbed. Why Greenway sent him to question a nurse was beyond him. Something about a fur coat which he was not supposed to mention.

Henderson wanted to be back pounding the pavement, checking out the beer joints, pool halls and the girls rolling the big fat cigars in the local cigar shops. That's where he belonged, where he felt he was needed, and more importantly appreciated.

He tugged on his coat. "I'd like to ask a few questions. May I come in?"

A chill clawed up her spine. "Of course. How can I help, officer?"

Henderson, being who he was, couldn't help notice Miss Trigby was an attractive woman with some nice curves on her.

"We understand you worked with Dr. Wolf at Agnew Sanitarium and Hospital. Pardon my bluntness, but we were given to understand he had inappropriate relationships with some of the nurses. Did you know about this or maybe heard gossip?"

"I doubt that ever happened, officer. Yes, I heard gossip. But I think that's all it was, just gossip. Like any high-stress job, people can be jealous and petty at times. So I didn't take any store in the whispers around the hospital." She tilted her head and smiled at the officer.

Henderson's eyes widened and he licked his lips. A telling, unconscious response Rose thought. This guy would be easy to wrap around her finger, but dangerous at the same time. Traits she was drawn to. A little flirting would keep him wondering instead of his mind on the job where it should be. She bet his opinions about women had been a minefield of misunderstandings since puberty. Probably ended up with many a slap across the face or worse.

"I was about to make some tea. Would you like a cup?"

"A glass of water would be good." He looked around the room and licked his lips again.

"Of course. I'll be just a minute." What an imbecile. As if she wouldn't know he was going to 'case the joint,' while she was in the kitchen. She was a big fan of Nick Carter, Master Detective, and avidly read all his dime-novel potboilers. She was well aware of all the tricks the coppers used.

Besides, the idiot would find nothing to tie her to Asa. She made sure of it. Her entire apartment had been carefully scoured of any association to Asa. Any evidence that would link her to Asa other than working with him at the hospital would be dangerous.

Well aware someone living on a nurse's salary might have a bottle of sherry, but certainly not expensive bourbon, she poured Asa's bourbon into two well-scoured vinegar bottles. The Waterford glasses were filled with bacon grease and left under the sink. Not that this oaf of a man would know Waterford from Shinola.

Photos and expensive lingerie had been cut up and tossed down the chute leading to the building's furnace. The fur coat went into the Salvation Army's collection box. It just about killed her to give it away, but there was no choice. A fur would look completely out of place in her closet. Not something a moral, upright, single working woman would own. She could only guess what the Salvation Army workers thought when they pulled it out and saw it. Wonder if they would appreciate it came from a premier New York furrier.

Officer Henderson swallowed his water in a swift gulp. "If you think of anything the police department should know, give me a call...Officer Henderson, Officer Bart Henderson."

"I'll do that Officer Henderson."

Henderson nodded and left.

The locksmith was standing in the kitchen doorway. "Did you give some thought about the plywood?"

"It sounds like a good idea, but I'd better check with the building manager first. I'll let you know."

The locksmith gathered his tools, wrote up a receipt, took his payment, and left.

Fixing a cup of her grandmother's herbal tea, Rose sat in the kitchen gathering her thoughts about her new 'romance.' The relationship seemed promising. Fayette Watkins was a good catch. Talk around the hospital was Watkins would assume Asa's position as head of surgery and perhaps his seat on the Board. That would seal her position. She'd work on a raise when things were right. Even better, Watkins wasn't a womanizer like Asa. This could be a long-term liaison.

Taking her white work stockings and underthings from the hamper she carried them to the sink in the drying porch. Turning on the hot water tap, she ran the water until it was scorching and added soap. Steam rose with the clean scent of Ivory and lavender soap.

The birds in the trees outside her apartment building were certainly enjoying the day. She listened to the chattering and felt a nice breeze coming through the screens. Sticking a couple of clothespins in her mouth, she hung her undies on the lines strung across the porch.

The tight knots between her shoulders and in her neck began to loosen. The new locks made her feel protected and safe. A lullaby remembered from years back came to mind, and she hummed as she worked.

It was always a pleasure to see her clothes hung on the lines to dry. It brought back memories of summers spent with her grandparents. Helping her grandmother in the vegetable garden was fun, but she loved helping her hang the wash. That was the time fabulous stories were told of great, great grandfather, Sir Joshua Trigby and his vast landholdings in Wales, and how he ran away from the family's castle and his responsibilities, became a ship's cook and laundryman, and sailed the world. Her mother said the stories were pure rubbish, but Rose adored the stories and asked to hear them over and over.

Grandpa, whose mug she cherished, spent his time reading and working on an endless supply of jigsaw puzzles. He suffered from miners' lung and wasn't able to work. But his hugs were massive and comforting. At night, the three of them played Chutes and Ladders or Old Maid until bedtime. Then she brushed her teeth, said her prayers, and was tucked into a comfy cot on the sleeping porch.

When fall came around, she dreaded the return to her parents. From September to June, it was constant bickering and arguing. Bill collectors knocked on the door at the end of every month. Looking back she could understand the stress her parents were under, but at the time she didn't. Escape came by reading books and counting the days before summer vacation.

The third Saturday in June, she would pack a small suitcase and take the trolley to the end of the line. Her grandparent's met her at the stop and walked her the short block to their place where sweet, tangy and cold lemonade waited on the front porch.

Abruptly a timer bussed reminding Rose to grab her purse and catch the trolley to Marston's for the hat sale and the grocers for vegetables and eggs. If she was quick enough, there'd still be time for a short nap before Dr. Watkins arrived for their dinner date.

* * *

The Weiss Hungarian Restaurant on 6th Street in Coronado was perfect for a romantic dinner. Fayette Watkins and Rose smiled across a small, candle-lit table.

Entranced! That was the word Watkins had been searching for to describe the boyish feelings he felt around Rose. Their weekend in Redondo Beach made him realize how much he cared for her. It was all a little scary. He told himself to slow down and take things carefully and thoughtfully.

She looked beautiful in the candlelight. "What did you think?"

"The food was delicious. The spices were new to me, but I thought they were wonderful."

"I'm so happy you agreed to try Hungarian food. Most people turn up their noses. But I eat Hungarian dishes as often as I can. This is one of my favorite places."

"So I noticed. Everyone seems to know you."

"You could say I'm a regular."

"I think it's really nice of you to bring me to your favorite place. The meal was delightful, but the apple soup was outstanding. Do you think they would give me the recipe?"

"We can ask Mrs. Weiss. She might let you have her recipe. If not, I'll ask my *nagymama* for a copy of hers."

"*Nagymama*?"

"The word means grandmother. A little secret. I'm a quarter Hungarian. My *nagymama*, came to America years ago as a young widow and started a restaurant in New York City. She met my grandfather, a starving tailor. *Nagymama* made sure he had a good meal each night and a glass of wine. When he was offered a good-paying position in San Diego, they married and moved here."

Rose sipped her *Tokaji aszú,* a dessert wine. The evening was perfect. Fayette Watkins was something special. What a lovely change from Asa. Even better was venturing out in public without worrying if people might see them together. If she didn't watch herself, she'd fall head over heels.

"Rose, what do you say we stop by the Blue Mouse Cabaret for a couple of drinks and listen to the music? Another place where I'm well known."

The Blue Mouse was even more romantic than the restaurant. Dr. Watkins and Rose held hands and listened to the small group playing mellow jazz and popular songs. Rose had never felt so safe and cared for in a relationship before. For once, it wasn't about money or advancing her job.

As Watkins paid the bill, the waitress touched his sleeve, "Sorry to hear about the death of your brother-in-law, Dr. Watkins."

"Thank you, Velma."

"Must have been a shock and so unexpected. How terrible for your sister. Please give her our condolences when you see her. "

"Yes, I will. Thank you for your concern." He opened the front door hoping they could escape before Velma said more.

"Will you tell her we miss having her and Dr. Wolf here? Such a charming couple. You could see they were so happy together. I hope she's working through all the grief as best as can be. I know it's difficult. Love like that is hard to find."

"Yes, yes. See you next time, Velma."

The ride home was silent and tense.

When Fayette parked his car in front of Rose's apartment, he thought it best to clear the air of Asa Wolf.

"Rose, we should talk about Asa…and my sister too. Better to air things out. It's a cloud hanging over us."

"I don't want to go into it, Fayette."

"I think we should."

"Have I ever asked about the women you dated?"

"No, but this is different. Don't pretend it isn't."

Rose sighed. "I'm not ready to discuss him. I may never be."

"Rose we need to face facts. Be reasonable, please."

"I can't. Sorry if it's not acceptable and doesn't work for you. I understand completely. Perhaps it's best we end things."

Fayette didn't know what to say. He felt blindsided, confused, and angry…very angry. He didn't trust himself to say more. It would have been ugly. He gripped the steering wheel, his knuckles white.

Watkins didn't exit the car to open the passenger door, so Rose opened it and stepped out. "I'll see myself in. Thank you for dinner and drinks."

Fayette stared straight ahead, put the car in gear and drove off into the darkness. Rose watched his car pick up speed and race past the corner street lights for several blocks. He turned right, tires squealing. She waited ten more minutes in case he changed his mind. He didn't.

* * *

Back in the apartment, Rose lit the stove and put the kettle on for tea. Removing the pins from her hair and undressing in the dark bedroom, she slipped into her robe and slippers.

Her precarious position at the hospital had frayed her nerves to the breaking point. And now this breakup with Fayette! Despite her best efforts, tears ran down her cheeks and soaked the lacy robe she'd bought for tonight. The plan had been for Fayette to stay over but leave early before her neighbors woke up. Besides, he had an operation scheduled at 8:00 a.m., on the dot. He was not one to be late.

She grabbed a hankie, dabbed at her tears and blew her nose. Eye-opening how one kind comment from Velma at the Blue Mouse had ruined an otherwise perfect evening. It forced Rose to see the future as clear as a pane of glass. She didn't like what she saw.

It was time to face facts. Her romance (if it could be called that) with Asa would always be a stumbling block as long as she was with Fayette. A relationship with him would always be tainted by his friendship and family ties with his deceased brother-in-law. Whenever Fayette met people who knew the two men, Wolf's name was bound to come up in conversation. It was predictable, unavoidable. Fayette may or may not care, but for Rose, it was a knife to the gut. Probably would always feel like a knife to the gut. Strange considering how much she hated Asa. But there it was.

Then there was Louise Wolf. The holidays were coming. Had Fayette planned to invite Rose to join his family for Thanksgiving dinner? Would she be able to handle a day of family fun with the widow Wolf in attendance? No. It was too soon. Way too soon.

For example, she found herself acting in unpredictable ways since Asa died. In a moment of utter folly, Rose went to the Wolf house two days ago. Standing across the street staring at the house, she couldn't come up with one good reason why she stood there. But she was frozen to the spot. She didn't go up to the door, just stared until the maid came out to ask if she needed help. That broke the spell.

Rose mumbled, "I just wanted to give Mrs. Wolf my condolences." Not the reason. There was no reason. But it sounded sensible.

"Mrs. Wolf isn't home, but I can give her a message. Do you have a calling card?"

"No, I don't have any with me. My name is Rose Trigby. I met her at the hospital. I worked with Dr. Wolf. She may not remember me."

The maid's face twitched. Then with the precision of a prison guard, turned, returned to the house, and closed the door without once looking back.

Rose sighed, laced her tea with bourbon from one of the vinegar bottles, and drank it slowly. There were undies still pinned to the line on the porch. But no hurry. They could wait until morning. Pouring the last few drops of Asa's bourbon in her empty cup she padded to bed.

Maybe she could get some sleep before morning. Nadine across the hall would be expecting to have tea and inspect the hats she bought earlier. And that newspaper gal wanted to talk to her on Sunday. That might be tricky. She needed to be on her toes with her.

She blew her nose, sipped the bourbon and slipped between the sheets. Yes, any future with Fayette Watkins looked bleak at best. But he would be missed. Not the greatest lover she'd known, but kind and generous.

As she drifted off to sleep, her last thought was how safe she felt now the locks had been changed.

CHAPTER 17

September 11, 1915

Bad dreams and indigestion kept her tossing and turning most of the night. At 4:30 she gave in and got up for the day. Coffee first and then scrambled eggs and toast.

While she ate breakfast, she gave herself a talking to. Breaking up with Fayette was not the end of the world. She would look on the bright side if she could think of a bright side. Nothing came to mind.

When things bothered her, she often wrote a list of pros and con. But this morning she was too exhausted to think about making a list. Too tired to think about anything.

Her eyes looked a mess, so she took a cucumber from the icebox and cut two slices. She sat on the sofa, leaned back, placed the slices on her eyes, and fell asleep. Two hours later she opened her eyes. The cucumber slices were on the floor, and she felt almost like her old self.

Looking at the clock, she saw there was time to bake a coffee cake before her neighbor, came to visit. Coffee cake would be a nice compliment to the hat inspection. She gathered the ingredients and decided to add raisins and almonds.

As she mixed the ingredients, she thought about the newspaperwoman coming to interview her tomorrow. Calling her at work asking for a time to talk when Rose was busy was kind of a dirty trick. At least that's how Rose saw it. Maybe she'd be uncooperative and send her on her way.

An unexpected rain began to fall. It was the first rain after a hot summer, and Rose watched with pleasure as drops splashed against the window. The moisture in the air would soothe the summer heat she thought and maybe her scattered emotions.

She put the coffee cake batter in the oven and decided it was past time to take her things down off the line. The undies and the porch smelled wonderful. The lavender perfumed soap she'd started mixing with the Ivory flakes had a lovely scent. Putting the laundry items back on the shelf, she noticed something tucked behind a tub of old borax soap bits she used for scrubbing the kitchen counters. It was a book dark with age and dirt. She picked it up and placed it on a towel.

The book looked old, should-be-in-a-museum old. It must have belonged to Asa. But why would he leave it on her screened-in porch? Easy access if she wasn't home? Opening the book to the first yellowed page she read: *Personalis ex Libro Francis Drake*. She gasped, and her heart skipped a beat. Obviously, the book had something to do with the Drake Research Society Asa had been involved with.

She didn't know the details, but she was well aware he and his friends had something illegal in the works. She'd met the other three men, all sketchy. Jeffery with the ridiculous beard, Ezra with the twitchy eye, and sketchiest of all, Simon Bennet who thought he was the greatest gift to women since Don Juan.

Using a rag, she turned a few pages. It was a gem. A weather beaten book full of handwritten notes...this latitude, that longitude, detailed weather notations, the initials NM (nautical miles?) followed by numbers, sailors who required disciplining, ports of call, a page where the writing was overlaid with blood. That was a nice touch she thought. A semi-legible, water-stained map was stuck between pages near the back cover.

In the living room, she pulled out a drawer from her small desk. Removing the red-covered *San Diego City and Country Directory*, she flipped through the pages looking for Bennet, Simon. Dollar signs danced in her head.

Lou Wolf stared out the French doors. An unexpected, late summer rain had created puddles on her patio. She watched the water dance as drops fell on the tiles. The dark, gloomy weather matched her mood. Turning back, she lit a cigarette, one of many habits she had recently taken up, and flipped through the latest *Harper's Bazaar*.

Her mind couldn't focus on the magazine. The insurance policy plagued her today, like most days. After more than two months, the coroner still declined to give a positive cause of death. The police wouldn't or couldn't explain why. Did they suspect foul play or suicide? No one would say. Because of that, the insurance company refused to pay until a firm cause of death had been confirmed and signed in ink on the Death Certificate. And, if the certificate didn't state "natural causes," she would be the loser. Who knew there were clauses in the insurance policy about murder and suicide? Hideous man that Coroner. Didn't he realize what stress he was putting her through? The problem was like a bucket of water held over her head. She wanted it to go away.

It wasn't as though she would be forced to live in a cardboard box in some dirty alley. Asa's Last Will & Testament named Lou as his only heir. That left her well off financially. Thankfully, Asa had been prudent with his investments. Lou was surprised to find she now owned a great deal of San Diego property which she intended to sell. The money from the sales would be invested in the stock market where she wouldn't have to worry about it. Asa always said the stock market was rock-solid, good as gold.

Asa's books had sold bringing a good sum. Even better, there had been three inquiries about the house and it wasn't yet officially on the market. Seems plenty of people in San Diego wanted an Irving Gill designed home. As much as she disliked the house, no one else would know her true opinion of the place. She wanted top dollar. Heaven forbid someone would think she wanted to dump it.

The grounds in the back needed some work though. She reminded herself to tell Gilbert to cut back the weeds and bushes down by the storage shed. It was beginning to look like a jungle back there. When people came by to look around the property, it should look neat and tidy. Well-maintained gardens and lawns led people to believe the house would also be well-maintained.

But first things first. The cause of death and insurance needed to be settled. If the coroner decided it was suicide or murder, it would be a mess. Her stomach did a little flip-flop. Things needed to be settled, wrapped up, shipshape. That's how she liked things. That's how things should be.

Beth appeared with a tray of hot tea and shortbread cookies. She set the tray down, poured tea for them both and sat next to Lou on the sofa.

"Thank you, Beth. Such a gloomy day and a nice cup of hot Earl Grey is perfect. I do hope this downpour stops. Lillian Russell's stage show and the new movie, *Camille*, start next week in Los Angeles. I don't want to miss either of them. Lillian Russell is still magnificent at the age of 55 I've heard. I can't imagine being so old. Gives me the shivers just thinking about it."

"I wouldn't worry about the weather. I'm sure it's just a practice rain before the official winter rains. By the time we take the train to Los Angeles, it should be drier than a cracker."

Lou took a sip of her tea and relaxed back in her chair. "You always think so positive. Wish I could be more like you."

"You are positive. Been that way as long as I've known you. But so much has been happening lately, it has to be wearing. Even a saint would find your situation unsettling. Tying up loose ends after the funeral and wrangling with the hospital over Asa's papers, it's no wonder you feel kind of miserable. Give it time. Things will fall into place, and you'll be back to your old happy, bubbly self. This trip to Los Angeles should pick up your spirits."

"Thank you, Beth Ann. I hope so. Well then, so encouraged, let's continue looking forward to our week in Los Angeles. Ridiculous I have to travel miles away from San Diego to have any fun. But I'd never hear the end of it if someone saw me enjoying myself and tattle to my parents. I can hear them now. 'What will people think? The family can't have such scandal, Lou. We raised you better.' Etc." She gave a little yawn and lit another cigarette.

Lou looked out at the rain. "You're right, it's letting up." She took another sip of her tea. "Let's stop by that wonderful tea and herb shop we found in Chinatown on our last trip. Your idea to visit during Chinese New Year was the best. So much fun with the firecrackers exploding, the drums, the parade and all. Heavens, I loved the huge dragon and the costumes. So much color and terribly exciting."

Beth started to say something but thought better of it. "Good idea. The green tea you like so much is almost gone. We can stock up on it."

Lou added more sugar to her cup. "Did your mom like the herbs you bought for her arthritis?"

"I think she did."

Lou stirred her tea letting the spoon click against the side of the cup. Something she enjoyed doing because it irritated her mother to no end. "Did you know Earl Grey was a philanderer? Just like my incredibly marvelous husband? But at least Mr. Grey had a good heart and helped abolish slavery in Britain."

"No, I hadn't heard that. Asa did have his good points, just not as many as you would have liked."

"His good points? I can't believe you, of all people, would defend the man. Besides his good points in no way made up for the nurses he used and tossed aside. The fact he forced them to quit their jobs when he was bored with them teed me off. Last year, one of those poor women appealed to me for help. Not much I could do other than help with living expenses until she found a new job."

"It's good Asa never found out about it. What with his temper."

Lou snorted. "He'd never lay a hand on me."

"Probably not, but lately his drinking was making him erratic."

"Tosh. My brothers would have beaten him to a pulp. They might appear as well-mannered gentlemen, but appearances can be deceiving. And Asa saw them in action when some half-plastered man made a crass remark about my décolletage. Asa knew better."

Beth said nothing. She and Lou grew up in the same household but in different parts of the house. Beth downstairs, the only child of the head housekeeper. Lou upstairs, the Watkins' only daughter. Headstrong and unruly from day one, Lou delighted in roughhousing with her three brothers. Such unladylike behavior was frowned upon by Mr. & Mrs. Watkins. They filled the playroom with a massive supply of board games, books, expensive dolls, child-sized tea sets, and a giant Victorian dollhouse. Beth was brought upstairs to help occupy their rambunctious offspring and to keep her busy and quiet in a ladylike manner.

As a consequence, Beth knew all Lou's dreams and naughty secrets. And there were many. But thankfully, she was loyal as the Watkins' cocker spaniels. Beth went so far as to accept the blame for Lou's often mischievous actions. Before long it became a habit, protecting Lou from her bad behavior. That, in turn, led to Lou not having the foggiest notion where the socially, acceptable lines were drawn.

Someone knocked at the door. Beth answered to see a delivery van and two men with a large traveling trunk from New York.

Lou stubbed out her cigarette. "How exciting. The dresses arrived in time. Hey, kiddo, let's get dolled up in my new clothes. The New York fashion house I like has a new designer and oh the colors he uses! Can't wait to see what he sent.

"Then we can open some ridiculously expensive wine, play some of my new dance records, and you can teach me the foxtrot. I've been playing at being a matron for so long, I've lost touch with what fun means anymore."

Beth grinned. "Great idea. Last one up the stairs is a rotten egg.

CHAPTER 18

September 12, 1915

The murderer stood in the kitchen and carefully thought through what to do next. Technically, it was not yet a murder. The victim was still breathing. But after all the things said and done in the last ten minutes, only one solution was left. Best to get it over with.

Stepping to the stove, the murderer twisted a nob, and gas hissed into the air. Life could be unfair, and too often was.

* * *

Sadie checked her notes. She was at the right apartment, but Rose Trigby wasn't answering her door. Her first thought was Rose had changed her mind about being interviewed for Sadie's article or perhaps she forgot and left for church or...

A door opened across the hall and an elderly lady peeked out.

"Miss? Are you looking for Rose Trigby? She may not be up yet."

"I had an appointment with her. I was to meet her here." Sadie had a bad feeling. It was almost Noon, the agreed-upon time. Someone as detail-oriented and precise as a nurse wouldn't forget an appointment. She hadn't seemed happy about agreeing to the interview, but if she changed her mind, she surely would have called or left a note on her apartment door. "When did you see her last?"

"Yesterday morning it was. She and I had tea and cake and examined the hats she bought from Marston's Department Store. Having a big sale they were." She smiled and showed Sadie her gnarled hands. "I used to be a milliner in my younger days before the arthritis got me and made a wreck of my fingers."

Sadie nodded politely.

"Soon as I finished my Bible studies this morning, I was going to knock on her door myself. She was a little down about her breakup with her new boyfriend. Just wanted to check on her."

Sadie's skin prickled with apprehension. "I had an appointment to meet her here at Noon. Does she usually sleep this late?"

"Oh my, is it Noon already? I was so involved in reading 'Revelations' didn't realize how late it's become. Well now, this is worrisome. She never sleeps in, even on her days off. So used to getting up early, she doesn't use an alarm. Although sometimes she has to work the midnight shift which she's not happy about, but that's the life of a... "

Sadie broke in. "It's Sunday. Any possibility she would be at church? Or maybe was called away?"

"I don't think so. Rose would have knocked on my door to tell me. Lately, she's been particular about telling me where she was going and when she'd be back. I don't know what it was, but something scared her a few months ago, enough to change her locks even."

"Should we get the manager to unlock her door and check on her?"

"She gave me a spare key. Let me get it."

The neighbor opened Rose's door. The smell of gas was strong. The neighbor covered her mouth and shuffled into Rose's kitchen to open the windows and the door into the screened-in porch. Sadie followed right behind and turned off the gas lever on the stove.

Judging by the mottled colors of her skin, the woman crumpled on the kitchen floor was beyond help.

Sadie propped open the screened porch door helping to clear out the gas. She and the neighbor returned to the hallway.

The woman had no phone. It was too expensive she said. Sadie found the manager at home and used his phone to call for help. He ran to Rose's apartment and then quickly left looking sick.

The neighbor sat on her sofa dabbing at tears. "Can't believe this happened to such a lovely person. She was always so careful, so exact about everything she did. Just goes to show even the most cautious people get distracted at times and do silly things. You don't think it was suicide, do you? No, surely not."

Sadie handed her another handkerchief. "Let me make you some coffee or some tea while we wait for the police."

"There's a fresh pot of coffee. I made it just before I heard you knock on poor Rose's door. Pour us both a cup, please. I take mine black."

Sadie found two cups, poured coffee and sat next to the neighbor.

"Here, have a sip. The police should be arriving soon."

"I feel awful. Sitting here reading 'Revelations" and all the time sweet Rose was dying across the hall. Not something I'll ever forget, you know what I mean?"

Sadie patted the neighbor's hand. "Don't feel guilty. By the looks of her, I'd guess she's been dead for some time. Probably before you woke up this morning."

The neighbor began sobbing. "It's so difficult to take in. I know she was terribly unhappy about breaking up with the new gent. He was sweet and kind...a doctor. Certain things couldn't be worked out, she said. But still, the new man wasn't like Dr. Wolf who wasn't a nice man, not at all. I have to admit I was relieved when he was found dead."

"Relieved? Why was that?

"I'm not one to speak ill of the dead, but he was full of himself. An arrogant man he was. He expected Rose to be at his beck and call. If she was, it was all wine and roses. If she wasn't, he had a fit. Bad-tempered you know. Men like him? It's only a matter of time before the woman ends up hurt or worse."

Sadie refilled their cups. "Well, it's good Rose had a kind neighbor such as yourself. I was told she was a good person and a terrific nurse."

"She was. She truly was. I'm going to miss her. Such a lovely person."

Sirens in the distance grew loud and stopped in front of the building. Three men from the fire brigade ran up the stairs and into Rose's apartment. After assuring themselves the gas was off, there were no leaks, and gas in the apartment had dissipated, they stepped across the hall into the neighbor's living room.

"Good job, ladies. We'll take it from here."

The police arrived and took statements from Sadie and the neighbor. Just as Sadie was leaving, Coroner Cohen arrived with his red notebook and held the lobby door for her.

He tipped his hat and took the stairs two steps at a time.

* * *

At the *Herald*, Sadie typed up a detailed story about the death of Rose Trigby and handed it to the managing editor with a copy to Max.

"Good job, Sadie. We'll run it in tonight's edition."

Face burning with excitement, Sadie grinned. "Thank you, sir. I appreciate it."

"This is your first article over and above your column, *Flying the Skies*, am I correct?"

"Yes, sir."

"Good to be at the right place, at the right time, hey?" He picked up a pencil and began editing.

That evening, Sadie unfolded her copy of the evening edition and was disappointed with the editor's treatment of her first newsworthy story. Not only was her article not on the front page, above or below the fold, but it was on the back page. Her title, *Herald Reporter Discovers Body of Agnew Sanitarium Nurse*, had been changed to *Nurse Found Dead*, and half the article had been edited away. The editor had given her a byline. At least that was a good thing. She shrugged. So it wasn't a front-page item, at least it was a beginning.

Resolute, she clipped the article and pasted it in a new green leather scrapbook with gold trim she had purchased that afternoon. Now she had a blue scrapbook for her column and a green scrapbook for her newspaper articles. The first of many articles she hoped. She felt official, kind of, almost. But she had a ways to go to catch up with the three scrapbooks and a box full of her grandfather's newspaper articles. Grandma Missy Brown had lovingly kept every Equal J. Brown newspaper story known to exist.

Sadie sat at her Underwood and finished typing out her conversation with Rose's neighbor. Interesting. She hadn't heard about Dr. Wolf's temper before.

CHAPTER 19

September 13, 1915

Dr. Watkins was the next person to be interviewed on Sadie's list. Besides being Wolf's brother-in-law, he had been a friend. He might have known Wolf better than anyone. She'd try for an appointment. If he agreed, all to the good. Showing up unexpectedly didn't seem to work with the hospital doctors, but she would resort to it if necessary.

She wanted to tread lightly in her questioning of Lafayette Watkins for two reasons. First, Sadie wanted to explain she was writing an unbiased and complimentary article of Dr. Wolf and his research. She wanted it known she wasn't on a witch hunt. If her plan worked, she hoped the rest of the hospital staff would treat her with less suspicion than in the past. Secondly, Watkins might be upset over Rose Trigby's death.

Whatever anyone thought, her article would be honest where ever the truth took her. And for many reasons, she wanted no one to suspect what she learned would go directly to the ear of Sergeant Greenway.

* * *

September 14, 1915

A haggard and red-eyed Dr. Watkins ushered Sadie into his office. Judging by his appearance, he had experienced a bad night.

"Sorry to keep you waiting, Miss Brown. It's been a very busy day today. So many people with lung problems moving to San Diego for our healthy weather. Seems they all head straight to our sanitarium first thing. But my busy schedule isn't what you came about. You're here to write an article about the late Dr. Wolf. I only have ten minutes or so to spend with you before my next patient, but I'm happy to tell you what I know about him. He was a good friend besides being my sister's husband." He plastered an encouraging smile on his ashen face.

"Thank you. I'll try to keep my questions to a minimum. First, may I ask how you came to meet Dr. Wolf?"

Watkins leaned back in his chair. "Ah yes. Quite the pleasant memory. It was at a weekend conference sponsored by a drugstore chain and a pharmaceuticals company."

She opened her notebook. "Here in San Diego?"

"No, no. Los Angeles." He paused. "Funny. I don't remember what drugs they were introducing. What stands out is meeting Asa. He was giving a lecture about combining drugs, baths, and electricity to help in the treatment of female hysteria. I introduced myself, and we spent the better part of the weekend discussing our mutual interests."

Sadie nodded and smiled encouragingly.

"I was looking for a new surgical position, and Asa recommended me to the hospital. And here I am...happily, I might add. It was later he met my sister, and we became brothers-in-law."

"How did he met your sister? Tennis tournament was it?"

"Yes, at a tennis tournament. He took an instant liking to Lou. She's a lovely, charming girl. Men have always been attracted to her. Before I knew it, they were announcing their engagement."

"And did your family approve...the age difference an all?"

"Well my parents were hesitant, but Asa was an excellent salesman as well as a top-notch surgeon. To tell you the truth, we were all under his spell. He had charisma. But you've probably heard that before."

Sadie smiled. "And the marriage was a good one?"

"Well, of course, every marriage has its ups and downs. But from what I could tell, both of them were quite happy. There was some dissension regarding the amount of time he spent away from home. He spent a good deal of time at the hospital. But that's a common issue with doctors' wives in general."

"Can you tell me about his experiments and research? That's going to be the thrust of my article, how Dr. Asa Wolf dedicated his life's work to helping humanity." Sadie wondered if that last comment might have been over the top, but Watkins didn't seem to think so.

"I am delighted to hear that. Wish I could help you, but he kept his research close to his chest. He did tell me and others at a recent party his next paper would be groundbreaking. He said he had some ideas for patents which would set him and Lou up financially for life. I think the hospital was interested to hear that too."

Sadie decided to take a guess. "I heard he owned a bunch of stocks and bonds."

"He may have. He didn't share his finances with me. But that would explain the big house and trips to Europe."

"I also heard his skills as a surgeon were top notch. But were there ever any problems or complaints about his experiments with electricity and female hysteria?"

He sat up straight and looked her in the eyes. "Never! Never a complaint! His reputation was spotless." He looked at his clock. "I best call an end to our talk. I have a patient waiting. It's been a pleasure. I can't wait to read the article."

"Thank you for your help and insight. Sounds like Dr. Wolf was a brilliant man. How fortunate to have known him so well."

Watkins stood and gave her a brittle smile. "Yes, he was brilliant. And yes, I was fortunate. If I can help in the future, let me know."

"Thank you. Perhaps you can suggest others who could give me more insight into his research?"

"As I said, he kept his research under wraps. No doubt you're aware, there's a legal issue between the hospital and Asa's estate about his papers and possible patents. I doubt anyone who works for the hospital would want to step into a quagmire between dueling legal teams."

So much for well laid-plans and cautious questions. "I can see people would be hesitant. So I doubly appreciate your help. Thank you again."

The interview had created more questions than answers. Groundbreaking research? Patents? Maybe some exploration in the *Herald's* archives would help.

Instead of using the building's elevators, Sadie took the stairs down to the street. She loved the thrill of flying but wasn't keen about elevators.

Watkins looked down to the street from his office window and replayed their conversation. He was positive he had said nothing to endanger himself. She was a nosey little thing but just a girl after all. Nothing to worry about. However, he thought it would be best if she gave up her article about Asa and disappeared or just disappeared period.

* * *

Elderly Mr. James in the *Herald's* archives was finishing his lunch, a corned beef and cheddar cheese on rye sandwich. A slice of home-made apple pie sat nested in waxed paper waiting to be consumed for dessert. His new electric kettle bubbled next to a teapot and mug, a gift from Mrs. James for their anniversary.

He was daydreaming about retirement when he heard footsteps descend the stairs. Looking up he spied the newspaper's only female writer. Slipping on his glasses, he wiped his hands on a napkin, smiled at Sadie and walked to the counter.

"Sadie. My favorite writer. How nice to see you. Are you looking for something for your column? I've been sifting through old papers about aviatrixes like you asked. Your focus on women in the world of flight is interesting. Something the other journalists around here ignore. Mrs. James and I find your writing special and highly underrated in our opinion."

Sadie wanted to hug Mr. James but held back. He wasn't the hugging type. But he was thoughtful and one of the kindest men she'd ever met. Also, he was the only person at the paper who thought of her as a writer, not a *female* columnist or a newspaper*woman*, but a newspaper writer.

"Thank you, Mr. James. How is Mrs. James? Still writing her cookbook?"

"Lucinda's fine. Just fine. She said to say thank you for the crate of apples you brought from Julian. Impossible to get perfectly ripe apples unless one has an apple tree in their yard or they live close to Julian." He pointed to a slice of pie waiting to be eaten with a cup of freshly brewed tea. "And as the beneficiary of Mrs. James' culinary expertise, I also say thank you. But I doubt you came to talk about apples. What's up?"

"I'm writing an article about Dr. Asa Wolf, the dead man they found back in July at the Expo."

Mr. James nodded his head but said nothing. He never interrupted or tried to second guess. He waited until people finished talking before he spoke. It had kept him out of hot water more than a few times. Dumb questions often popped in his head, but he counted to ten before opening his mouth.

"I'm wondering if there were ever any lawsuits or public complaints about Agnew Sanitarium and Asa Wolf in particular."

"I don't recall a lawsuit involving Dr. Wolf in particular. However, I'm sure there must have been. I can't think of a doctor in San Diego hasn't had their share of unhappy patients and families. I remember when Dr. Wolf began working for Agnew and his first wife's untimely death. I can start..."

"Wait. What first wife?" Sadie had no compulsion about interrupting others. A habit her grandmother had long tried to break her of.

"Oh yes. Katherine Wolf. It was a sad case. She was quite young and expecting their first child. I don't remember the exact details. Something to do with electricity. I do remember the date. Would you like me to pull the article now or would you rather come back later after I do some research about hospital lawsuits and complaints involving Dr. Wolf?"

"I'd like to see the paper about her death now if you wouldn't mind."

"Of course." Mr. James walked to his desk, took a quick sip of his tea and then walked into the depths of the archives, back ramrod straight as the day he started working for the *Herald* when he was twenty-one.

As long as he could remember, he had a gift for memory. Association was the key, but he was unable to explain to others how it worked. And now the date of July 7, 1901, flashed in his mind surrounded by the colors always associated with the different months and numbers. He found the papers in question and brought them to the counter where Sadie was signing the request log.

"I brought the papers from the 7th to the 26th. There were several articles due to an investigation. The police had their suspicions. This stack should cover it."

"Thank you and your amazing memory, Mr. James. Please, finish your lunch. I'll look through these and come back later to check on the articles about complaints. Would you put a note in my mail slot when you finish with your search?"

"Of course."

"And next time I drop off my column, I'll bring a few jars of Fallbrook's world-famous honey. There's a group of ladies in Fallbrook who keeps bees. They wrote to bribe me with a promise of honey if I would join them for lunch and mention them in my column. We set a lunch date for tomorrow at Fallbrook's Ellis Hotel."

"Mrs. James will be thrilled. She's a big fan of Fallbrook's honey and we purchase the olive oil from there too. Any honey you want to gift us with will be put to good use. Thank you, Sadie. Thoughtful as always."

Sadie smiled. She wished other people at the *Herald* thought so. But it would take more than honey to gain her editor's attention. She saw a maze ahead full of disappointing dead-ends before she had her story ready for his approval.

The room was silent except for Mr. James sipping his tea and savoring his apple pie while Sadie gently flipped the flimsy newsprint and wrote notes. She couldn't believe what she was reading. Did Dr. Wolf get away with murder?

CHAPTER 20

September 15, 1915

The sun was burning through the last of the morning overcast when Sadie stepped from the train at the DeLuz/Fallbrook station. Gratefully, she took several deep breaths of cool, clean air. The passenger car had been overheated and smoky. Opening a window meant dealing with smoke and cinders from the engine.

She thought about her day ahead. Clearing her head of Wolf's murder had become a necessity. She was close to becoming obsessed. Lunch and interviewing the beekeeper ladies was the perfect antidote.

Being an investigative reporter made for sleepless nights. She found it difficult to turn her mind off lying in bed at night. It would have been a boon to mankind if humans had been created with an on-and-off switch for the brain. Seriously, in Sadie's opinion, God had made a grave miss-step there.

In the small parking area, a livery wagon stood ready to gather passengers and ferry them into town. Sadie smoothed out her pale blue linen walking suit, gathered her parasol, straw hat, folio, and prepared to step into the wagon but was stopped short.

"Miss Brown. Miss Brown." A little girl of perhaps six years was running towards her calling her name.

"Miss Brown. My mother and my brother are over there in the buggy." She pointed at the station's loading dock where a buggy hitched to a pair of matching Bays was parked. A teenage boy was discussing a stack of boxes with the station master while his mother, a dark-haired woman, sat straight-backed next to him in the buggy. She smiled and lifted a gloved hand to wave.

"We're sending olive oil and honey to Oceanside. Soon as they're done, we'll drive you and mommy to the hotel." The girl took Sadie's hand, and they walked to the buggy.

"Beautiful markings on your Bays," Sadie remarked.

The boy signed off on the freight bill. "You have a fine eye for horses, Miss Brown."

"My father taught me how to appreciate all animals but horses in particular." After introductions, the boy helped Sadie into the buggy, and the Bays easily pulled the buggy up the hill into the town of Fallbrook.

The woman smiled and asked about Sadie's train ride from San Diego and about the Exposition. She and her family planned to visit the Expo in the fall if the harvest cooperated.

Coming into town, Sadie saw the Victorian era styled Ellis Hotel immediately. The dove gray hotel's shingled red roof and dormers were crowned with a red and white turret making it stand out against the dry summer grasses. It looked like a confectioner's delicious dream of frosting and peppermint candy.

The beekeeper ladies waited on the veranda dressed in their summer best. To have a lady reporter from San Diego in their midst and an aviatrix to boot was a treat. They had more questions about Sadie than she had for them.

Settled around a large table in the dining room, the ladies gratefully removed their gloves. The day was getting warmer by the minute. As they waited for their lunches, Sadie filled her notebook with questions and answers. In her opinion, writing a successful column meant gathering enough information for five columns. Her biggest problem was paring the article down to the size her column was allowed. The beekeepers took turns answering her queries.

"Yes, it's very profitable. We sell thousands of pounds of processed honey, frames of honey, and beeswax every year. Olive oil is a big moneymaker in Fallbrook, but we give them a run for their money."

"The bees love just about anything that blooms. Someone planted an experimental grove of avocado trees three years ago. Now the bees have plenty of choices...olives, lemons, and avocados. The bees seem happy and so are we."

"Oh yes, you heard right about the health benefits. Truly amazing. Honey's well known for what ails you, sore throats, fevers, aids digestion, you name it. My mother swears by a poultice of minced onions and honey on any kind of wound."

"Bee stings? Oh most certainly." Each woman around the table nodded in agreement. "We have all suffered a bee sting here and there. But for the most part, the bees are calmer when women are around than when the menfolk are. Personally, I like to move in a peaceful manner and hum my favorite hymns while I work with the hives. The bees like it and so do I."

"Family? My daughter plans to continue keeping bees, but my son wants to raise cattle. Reads too many Zane Grey books if you ask me. But some children need to break away from family and small-town life. There are those, like my Jamie, that just have to make their own way."

Sadie closed her notebook as their salads arrived.

Over iced tea and dessert, a delicious spice/honey/lemon cake topped with sugared lemon blossoms and sprinkled with crystalized slivers of honey, the ladies bombarded Sadie with their own questions.

"So, Miss Brown, tell us about yourself...how you became a journalist and what it's like being up in the sky, thousands of feet above the ground, in one of those flying machines. Sounds terrifying.

Sadie added sugar to her iced tea. "Not that much to tell. My desire to be a reporter comes from my grandfather, Equal J. Brown. He was an investigative journalist in San Francisco. The writing bug skipped my father evidently, because other than keeping notes in his journal, my father preferred banking as a career.

"When I was younger, I liked to write little books and plays. But writing wasn't something I was serious about until my parents were killed in an earthquake, the one in San Francisco. I was sixteen. It rattled my life and made me take a close look at what I wanted to accomplish. So I decided to get serious about my writing and began to study journalism.

"As for flying, a friend and I visited Coronado to watch an air meet at the Polo Grounds. All those aeroplanes? It was perhaps the most thrilling thing I had ever seen. My heart was about to burst from excitement. I was hooked.

"I visited a flying school and by helping them here and there, earned enough money to take lessons. That's when I cut my hair so my goggles and leather hat were easier to put on and take off. My grandparents were horrified. Lucky for me, my understanding boyfriend says I look pretty either way, long or short hair. He was the one who suggested I write a column about flying. *The Herald* gave me a chance, and that's how I ended up having lunch with a group of lady beekeepers today."

The ladies were thrilled to hear her simple life story. Even the waitresses had joined the group to listen. To Sadie, working with bees sounded more dangerous than flying. She had control of her aeroplane, but bees had a mind of their own. All a matter of perspective.

"Would you all like to know a little secret?"

"Yes. Of course, we would." The ladies fanned themselves and sipped their ice tea.

"First, I must swear you to secrecy. Only my boyfriend knows what I'm going to tell you." She leaned forward. "I'm working on my first investigative story, and it's about a murder." Sadie sat up straight wondering why she was sharing this with a group of ladies she had just met.

There were murmurs of surprise, promises to never tell another soul, and more fanning. The beekeepers sat forward.

"A well-known San Diego surgeon was found dead in one of the exhibit buildings in Balboa Park last July. At first, it appeared to be a heart attack, but some strange details made the police believe it was murder. I've taken it on myself to follow a whole maze of clues, which I hope will lead me to the killer and the motive. And when I do, I plan to write an investigative story and see the murderer brought to justice." Sadie sat back wondering what had gotten into her, yapping on about Dr. Wolf's murder. She wished she could take it all back, but it was too late now.

She smiled. "Enough of that. Let's get back to the Fallbrook beekeeper column I plan to write. Instead of being about aviators and aviatrixes, I plan for it to be one-hundred percent about the tiny but mighty bee, how it flies, and how the beekeeper makes its life better. Should be in the *Herald* in two weeks."

She took a last bite of cake, drank what was left of her iced tea, and checked her watch. "I'd better be getting back to the station before I miss my train. You have all been a delight to meet and interview. It's going to make a wonderful column. Thank you so much."

One of the ladies had a motorcar and drove Sadie to the station.

"Thank you for joining us for lunch. We haven't had such fun since can't remember when. Like we promised, here are some jars of honey to take home with you." The woman suddenly looked serious.

"Miss Brown. Please, before you go, I want to ask a question."

"Of course. What would you like to know?"

"Was it Dr. Asa Wolf who was murdered?"

"Yes. Did you read about his body being found back in July?"

"Yes. I didn't know it was murder, but I'm not surprised. He's hurt people, myself included. I'm glad someone stopped him from hurting others."

"He hurt you? Did you file a complaint?"

"Yes, he did. But I didn't file a complaint. I couldn't. My family, my friends, no one knows anything. If they did, it would be the end of me. You're the only person I've told."

Tears were forming in her eyes. "Have a good trip home, Miss Brown. Thank you for listening to my secret."

Sadie gripped her hand. "Your secret's safe with me."

"And yours with me."

The engine gave a sharp whistle. The conductor yelled. "All aboard for Oceanside. Connections to southbound trains to San Diego and northbound to Los Angeles at the final stop."

Sadie stood with one foot on the coach step. "Are you okay now? I mean, are you well?"

She took a swipe at her eyes and tried a smile. "Yes. I'm well now. But I hope you don't find the killer. Whoever did it deserves a medal. Goodbye, Miss Brown."

The train lurched, steam hissed, and the conductor shooed Sadie into the car. When she got to a seat and looked out the window, the young woman was gone, but her face and what she said were burned into Sadie's brain.

CHAPTER 21

September 16, 1915

At 8:00 a.m. Sadie stood on the Wolf's doorstep. She knocked softly hoping Lou Wolf would still be sleeping. It was Beth she wanted to speak with.

Beth opened the door a crack and whispered. "Miss Brown. What are you doing here so early?" Beth's whispered question made it plain Lou was still tucked in her bed asleep.

Sadie whispered back. "I'm so sorry to bother, but I was hoping to ask you a few more questions. I've come across something a little sensitive and didn't want to disturb Mrs. Wolf with my inquiry."

Beth motioned Sadie inside. "Mrs. Wolf is still sleeping. She's been exhausted since her husband's death. There's been an unbelievable amount of stress tending to the estate." She tipped her head towards the back of the house. "Come to the kitchen. I just fixed a pot of coffee. The cook isn't due to work for another hour, so we'll have the kitchen to ourselves."

The stark, modern kitchen was brilliantly lit with sunshine streaming through large windows. Beth filled two cups with coffee and motioned Sadie to the breakfast nook. In spite of the stark and understated kitchen, the nook was warm and cozy.

"So, what are your questions? I mean, I don't know what more I can tell you. Mrs. Wolf is my friend as well as my boss. I don't want to get more involved than what I've already shared."

"It's about an article I found in the *Herald's* archives. What do you know about Dr. Wolf's first wife and her death fourteen years ago? Do you know anything about the circumstances?"

Sadie wasn't sure, but for a fraction of a second Beth looked surprised or maybe it was a look of relief. The look came and went so quickly, Sadie couldn't decide.

"Very little. I was still a kid back then, but I do remember my mother talking about it. Lots of ugly rumors were floating around back then about Dr. Wolf. But he was never charged with anything. Pretty sure Mrs. Wolf's death was declared an accidental electrocution. I'm glad you weren't planning to ask Lou about this. She doesn't need more upset in her life right now...especially over something that happened years ago. But maybe you should talk with, Gilbert."

"Gilbert?"

"Gilbert Shine, the family's chauffeur. He's was Asa's driver for a long time. Well before Asa met Lou."

"Interesting. Does he live on the property?"

"Yes. Over the garage. Can I suggest? Wait to talk with him until this weekend. Mrs. Wolf and I are taking the train to Los Angeles Friday and won't be back until Monday. That way, Mrs. Wolf won't know you were here. After you left last time, she was stressed for the rest of the day.

"Gil said he plans to spend the weekend working in the garden. It's a pet project of his. So he should be around whenever you stop by.

"And a big favor? When you talk with him, would you please not mention we spoke except at Fred Harvey's? Just say you stopped to talk to me, that you didn't know I'd be gone? Or something like that?"

"Okay, a little white lie now and then never hurts. Thank you for the coffee, Beth."

"And thank you for talking to me first."

"Mrs. Wolf is lucky to have you as an employee and a friend."

As Sadie left, she wondered about Beth's brief look. Was it surprise or relief? At every turn, there seemed to be secrets that needed sorting. Was no one capable of giving her straight answers? Something important was circling like a shark below the surface. She felt it and planned to ferret it out.

* * *

"Mr. James. I'm bringing gifts. Fallbrook honey." She placed a bag with five jars on the archive department counter.

"Was it a successful visit?"

"Very. I needed a break, and the trip was perfect to get my mind off Asa Wolf. That little town is still an unspoiled area. No liquor or spirits and no airfield, but I won't hold it against the place."

He chuckled. "I'm happy to hear that." He checked out the bag. "Five jars? Mrs. James will be delighted. Thank you so much, Sadie. Also, Mrs. James asked for all the details about the lunch the hotel served. You know how she is wanting every little detail when it comes to food?"

"We dined on Salad Nicoise which was excellent, perfect on a warm September day. The service was nicely done I might add. Ah, but the dessert, it was to die for. I don't remember if it had a name but it was a spiced-lemon-honey cake decorated with sugared lemon blossoms and crystalized honey bits."

"Oh yes, we've had it before. I agree. It's a special cake. Mrs. James near swooned over the taste and asked for the recipe, but the chef said it was an old family secret. Mrs. James keeps experimenting but hasn't found the exact ingredients and measurements yet. I may have to buy larger trousers before she figures it all out. But I'm enjoying all the 'failed' results.

"By the way, good timing with your visit. I was about to write you a note and put it in your mail slot. If you have a moment, I have an advertisement I think you'll find interesting. Seems Dr. Wolf was part of a group selling a 'newly-discovered' Francis Drake logbook and treasure map. Wolf was touting himself as an expert on ancient maritime history. Had the sound of a scam to me."

"Mr. James you are a jewel."

* * *

September 16, 1915

Lou Wolf was packing for her long weekend in Los Angeles. Seeking the opinion of a renowned eye specialist she told her family. The doctor touts certain vitamins contained in raw vegetables and a regime of eye exercises that are guaranteed to prevent the need for eyeglasses. In reality, she was desperate to get out of San Diego where people knew her. She wanted out of her widow's weeds if only for three days.

The proper mourning attire for the death of a husband, worn out of decency and respect, had quickly become tiresome. Her mother had been explicit: deep mourning for the first year dictated black silk & crape clothing with a black veil; second year purple was allowed and she could dispense with the black veil. Lastly, six months of normal clothing as long as it was dark in color. How utterly boring.

Her mother kept a copy close at hand of the *Household Companion Book of Etiquette* to use as a backup for her hard-held opinions. In her mind, etiquette is black and white. No exceptions. Etiquette is what keeps the world in check.

At the ripe old age of 25, Lou found mourning attire irksome after a week. Her mother was quite exasperated with her only daughter who was falling back into her old ways. It was worrisome. Life had been much easier when Lou was under the watchful eye of her son-in-law. He kept her reined in. Lord only knows what the future would bring.

Lou sat at her vanity and watched Beth pack the newly arrived fall dresses in her traveling trunk. Each one was a vision in shades of rust, green and a vibrant royal blue. Lou had no intention of letting the dresses go to waste just because she was a new widow. She watched with mounting pleasure as Beth carefully smoothed

139

out pieces of tissue and neatly wrapped each dress. The sound of the tissue was lovely and filled her with expectation. Since Asa's demise, the old cravings for fun and excitement were flooding back.

Lou nosily rattled and flipped the *Los Angeles Daily News* open to the amusements page. Pretending it was a big surprise, she screamed: "Beth, how exciting! Juliette Pascal and her Paris Garden orchestra are appearing at The Orpheum."

"What?" Beth grabbed the paper. "Forget it! Not going to happen, Lou. You remember what happened last time we met up with Miss Pascal? We were lucky to get out of New York with a slap on the hand from the police. Thank God Asa never heard. You would have been locked in your room for I don't know how long." Her stern face turned into a smile. "But the Italian guy, her dance partner, was adorable. He'd easily make it in motion pictures. Better looking than Douglas Fairbanks if you ask me."

"Rudy was a handsome one. Last I read, she's moved on to a new dance partner. Won't it be fun to see her again? Even better there's an Irish tenor on the bill. Won't that be heavenly, Juliette Pascal and an Irish tenor in the same program? You've always had a soft spot for Irish singers."

Beth shrugged. "I can't say it wouldn't be fun. Oh, you. You always know how to talk me into things we shouldn't be doing. Okay, but let's keep out of trouble this time. Please?"

Lou laughed. "Silly. One would think you were my mother sometimes, Heaven forbid. Why don't you pick out two or three of my Paul Poiret dresses from last year to wear? Though with hemlines going up, you'll need to take up the hems a little."

She looked at her shoe collection. Pumps now outnumbered the high-buttoned ones. With ankles on full display, high-button shoes had become passé. "You'll need some new pumps. We'll stop at Bloomingdales when we get to Los Angeles. Their shoe department is like a candy store. One can never have enough shoes. And Beth? You may as well keep the dresses. They'll be completely outdated by the time my mourning is over with.

"This is going to be so much fun. My heart is racing already!"

CHAPTER 22

September 17, 1915

On the train to Los Angeles, the ladies enjoyed lunch and reminisced about their last trip to New York. In 1914, with the war raging, traveling to Europe to buy from Paris designers Coco Chanel and Paul Poiret was out of the question.

So that year, Lou made appointments with several high-end fashion designers in New York. She couldn't help but notice Asa found it difficult to look unhappy he'd have to 'batch' it for a week. Not that she cared.

In New York, a designer recommended Juliette Pascal's show at the rooftop Paris Garden Club. Lou and Beth had watched captivated by Pascal and her Italian dance partner, a chap by the name of Valentino, glide across the floor while the Paris Garden orchestra played a sexy Argentine Tango.

The couple invited Lou and Beth backstage for drinks after their last performance. Several dancers from other stage shows were already backstage having a grand time. Lou and Beth joined in. The evening progressed rapidly until Lou and two dancers from the Ziegfeld Follies were arrested for breaking a variety of laws. Embarrassingly, it was in full view outside the Winter Garden Building.

Lou tried to explain to the police the dancers were teaching her a complicated dance step. It was why she had fallen on her bottom and was laughing so hard she couldn't stand up. The other two might be drunk, but she wasn't, honest.

The police had heard it all before and carted everyone off to the station. After an hour, Lou was released. The police told her to keep out of trouble for the remainder of her trip. If not, they wouldn't be so forgiving the second time around. Beth was waiting in the lobby of the station and was flooded with relief when Lou ambled out of the back looking chipper and trying to re-pin her hair.

"Beth, help me with my hair and see if they can find my shoes? Must be in that ridiculous room with all the drunks."

Following the brief stay in police custody and suffering an enormous hangover, Lou managed to rein in her enthusiasm for New York City's nightlife. Making the rounds of the designers she filled three trunks with dresses and millinery.

"It's more than I need, but I can't chose. Too many decisions. Besides, haven't I always lived by the motto it's impossible to own too many dresses, hats and shoes?"

* * *

A Beverly Hills Hotel driver and limousine were waiting at Union Station for the two women. They had reserved one of the new bungalows tucked in the back of the hotel. The cottage was perfect for two women looking for privacy and not wanting to traipse through the lobby coming and going.

They checked in at the desk and were escorted by two bellboys to their cottage. After a quick change, they readied themselves for dinner and the 10:00 p.m. show at the Orpheum.

Lou gave an usher a note for Miss Pascal. A return note came back inviting both ladies backstage after the orchestra had finished the last show. Opening the dressing door after a quick knock, they saw Juliette. She was removing her stage makeup but motioned Lou and Beth to enter. "I'm so surprised to see you! Give me a hug, honey. Does your husband know you're here?"

"No. He's not with us any longer. What I mean is..." She did her best to look somber. "He died of a heart attack this past July."

"I'm so sorry. Truly I am. But then again, I won't have to worry about hooligans busting into my dressing room and breaking my legs. Something your husband threatened to do if I ever met up with you again."

"What do you mean?"

"He sent a couple of thugs to the theater in New York after you left for home. They threatened to break some bones if I ever enticed you to 'run wild' as they put it, ever again."

"But he didn't know I was arrested."

"Oh, he most certainly did. The police called him the night they hauled you in. He and his influence are why you were let go with only a hand slap. Didn't he say anything when you got back to San Diego?"

"Not a word. He was just happy to see me and joked about how much money I spent on clothes."

"Well doesn't that beat all? I'll never understand men. It's been a problem since I could tell the difference between boys and girls." She laughed at her joke. Her latest dance partner rolled his eyes but didn't crack a smile.

* * *

September 18, 1915

One of Chinatown's larger tea shops, Wong's Tea, Herb, and Novelty was bustling with customers when Lou, Beth, and Juliette entered. The scent of sandalwood incense mingled with the smells of dried frog, fish, herbs and a slight hint of mothballs.

Juliette headed straight for a rack of brilliantly colored silk clothing. "How fabulous! I can't wait to try these on."

Lou stood at a long counter in front of shelves stacked with containers of tea. "Are you always this busy?" she asked the young man behind the counter.

The clerk, a handsome Chinese man smiled. "I wish. Most everyone you see here is getting ready for the Mid-Autumn Festival. Which means we're having a sale to bring extra customers in our doors. We always have sales just before holidays.

My grandparents arrived in San Francisco in the mid-1800s with five crates of tea and herbs. They began promoting their business by using holiday and festival sales. Now it's a family tradition."

"Sounds like a fascinating story."

"I think so." His eyes were fastened on Lou's.

She giggled. "Well, then." She felt her cheeks burning. "I'd like to hear the story sometime. For now, I'm here to purchase tea, green tea. I visited your shop last February, and I purchased an assortment. I'm almost out of the jasmine green tea, and I'd like to buy more. Can you help me?"

She felt a rise of excitement. The clerk hadn't taken his eyes from her. His eyes were amazing and they were staring straight into her own. She took a deep breath. It was as though she were coming up for air after diving into a deep lake. Her fingers tucked a stray lock of hair behind her ear, and she giggled again.

He grinned good-naturedly. "I'd be delighted. And may I suggest our white tea which arrived last week. It's a little more expensive but well worth the extra money."

Beth walked to the back where the herbalist was creating custom packets of aromatic herbs for customers.

"I'd like a package of herbs for my mother's arthritis." She gave the elderly woman the age, weight, and height of her mother. As she waited for the concoction to be prepared, Beth walked over to the dried fish and other dried items labeled with Chinese characters.

When the woman gave Beth the package, she tilted her head. "I remember you from before."

"I don't recollect meeting you before, but my employer likes to buy tea here whenever we visit Los Angeles."

The woman nodded solemnly. "Yes, of course."

The three ladies were all smiles as they left with their packages and headed toward the China Wall Cafe. Juliette had purchased a red silk-brocade dress and a black tunic embroidered with gold threads. Beth had her herbs and Lou her tea.

As they exited, Lou turned and waved at the young man. She skipped a step and turned. "Girls! We have been invited to an after-hours club tonight." She held up three chips for the Wong Sing Club. "It's a locals-only nightclub put up in a warehouse."

Juliette took a chip. "What the heck? Did you make goo-goo eyes at that gorgeous man?" She turned it over. "Looks legit. But I don't know. I'll have to think about it. I don't want to end up locked in some smoke-filled opium den. "

"Oh heavens, Juliette. That's ridiculous. You've been reading too many murder mystery novels. Danny invited us. He's going to sing tonight, and he wants you especially to see his set. It's not like we're going to be shanghaied into a life of sexual slavery or something."

Juliette laughed. "Danny? You work fast. On the other hand, using me to further his career makes me think he's probably on the up and up. Okay, I'm in. Could be a ton of fun actually. But, I am going to bring my partner. Just being cautious."

Lou slipped her hand in her pocket and pulled out a fourth chip. "Thank you. You're a doll. I told Danny you might want to bring Jose. So he gave me an extra chip."

* * *

Streetlamps pooled golden light on the corner of Shanghai and Jade. Lee Sing Import/Export warehouse was in some measure lit by the streetlights and the company's large neon sign. A man in a tight, dark suit which managed to showcase his muscular build without ripping the seams blocked the top of a stairwell leading down into the basement level. He lit a cigarette and tossed the match into the gutter.

"Ladies...and gent. You're out late. Need directions?"

Jose stepped forward and handed the man the four chips.

He squinted at them and nodded. "You must be Danny's friends. *Huanyng*. Welcome. The opera group is just finishing. Danny's on next." He pressed a button and stepped aside for them to walk down the semi-dark steps. "Wait a second for the door down there to open. Helps with the light. Don't want you to fall on your behinds." As promised, a door swung open at the bottom of the stairs allowing loud clapping and light to escape.

Inside a large partitioned-off room, small tables filled a semi-lit, smoke-filled space. On an intimate-sized stage in a pool of theatrical lighting, three male singers dressed in spectacular silk clothing, and wearing exotic makeup bowed to enthusiastic applause. The accompanying musicians removed their instruments from the stage and a drum set and a piano were rolled on.

Jose and the ladies were shown to a table in front of the stage. A small 'reserved' card was removed.

"Danny said the drinks are on him. So what'll you have?'

They ordered and watched as an announcer appeared on stage and spoke in Chinese. The crowd clapped and Danny and his banjo appeared from behind a red velvet curtain.

He sang two songs in Chinese and then a current popular melody, *I'm On My Way to Mandala.*

Lou nudged Juliette. "Wow. He's good don't you think?"

Juliette nodded. "I may have discovered a new singer for my Paris Garden Review."

* * *

The following day, the tickets to Lillian Russell's stage performance and the movie, *Camille,* lay on a table in the bungalow. They had been paid for but went unused. Lou planned to spend the day in Chinatown with Danny. Juliette rehearsed her orchestra and sent Danny Wong's card to her agent with a glowing recommendation.

Beth had plans too. She bought a copy of Mary Roberts Rinehart's latest mystery novel, *The Street of Seven Stars*, at the hotel's gift shop. Her plans were to read and stuff herself with food on the Bungalow's private patio. But first breakfast in bed followed by a lavish bath scented with the hotel's complimentary bath oil.

For Beth, this day would be pure luxury. A day filled with extravagance was something that had never happened in her limited life as a maid. As much as she adored Lou, too much perhaps, Beth seldom had time to herself, something she often begrudged. And when she did have a few free hours, the time was never used to indulge herself.

She called the front desk. "Hello? This is Bungalow 3. Connect me to room service." A cheery woman's voice answered. "Room service. How may we help?"

"This is Bungalow 3. Send over an order of French toast and bacon, a bowl of fruit and a pot of coffee." It took all Beth had to keep from saying *please, thank you* or *ma'am*. She ordered just as she had heard Lou and her family speak to people they considered servants or less.

"Right away, Miss."

Beth leaned back against a stack of feather pillows. This was going to be a day to remember.

CHAPTER 23

September 19, 1915

Gilbert Shine knelt in the garden and relished the sun working its hot fingers deep into his aching muscles. Good to be out from under the thumb of his employer if only for a few days. But working in the garden yesterday and today was taking a toll. He needed to do more grunt work, dig in the dirt, cut back shrubs, and pull weeds.

Gilbert saw it in the mirror each morning when he shaved. The towel tied around his middle couldn't hide his middle-aged body. It was getting soft and out of shape.

His knees especially felt the pain. Getting up and down with damaged kneecaps became more and more difficult with age. Running with a gang in his younger days offering no protection when a rival gang caught him alone in the wrong neighborhood. They dragged him into an alley. He was warned to stay out their territory by a solid swing of a baseball bat to his knees. Even though he got the message, the gang added a broken nose for good measure.

In spite of his knees and his flabby midsection, weeds had been pulled and bushes trimmed in the back of the property. Now he could enjoy himself with trays and pots of new plants waiting to be put in the earth. A large pile of spindly half-dead annuals had been tossed roots naked on a tarp. They had been replaced with new fall-blooming plants. He had made a head start on the heliotrope replacing the rangy, gone-past summer plants with a fall version when he heard footsteps.

"The heliotropes are beautiful."

Gil turned to see an attractive young woman regarding the plants.

"Mrs. Wolf has a passion for the plant's scent, and the hummingbirds can't get enough of the nectar. A plant that makes everyone happy, especially if you like purple."

He stood and removed his gardening gloves. "Mrs. Wolf is not at home. May I take a message?"

Sadie handed him her card and smiled. "I'm Sadie Brown. I'm writing an article for the *Herald* about Asa Wolf's research and humanitarian work."

"Humanitarian? Interesting. Like I said Mrs. Wolf isn't home."

"I've already spoken with Mrs. Wolf. I'm here to talk to you. Can you take a break from planting?"

"Me? Why?"

"Someone at the paper mentioned Dr. Wolf's first wife and her unusual death. I was wondering if you were their driver at the time."

"And did that someone at the paper mention the first Mrs. Wolf was my sister?"

Sadie felt her cheeks burn. She stumbled through the words. "I am so very sorry Mr. Shine. I had no idea."

Gil stared at the embarrassed girl and wiped away the sweat on his forehead. This Miss Brown wasn't a bad person he supposed. He shouldn't have made her feel awkward. Always the knight in shining armor he chided himself. "I see that. Here, have a seat in the shade, and I'll pour us some lemonade. I'll tell you what I know about Dr. Wolf for your article, but I'd rather not go into detail about my sister, Katie."

Sadie let out the breath she'd been holding. "Thank you, Mr. Shine. I'd appreciate anything you wish to share."

The two moved next to the garage where a small patio and a seating area had been placed behind a screen of camellia bushes.

Sadie noticed outside stairs leading to a second story. Must be the man's living quarters she surmised. Sitting in the shade was a relief. And it was a bigger relief the man hadn't kicked her off the property after she put her foot in her mouth about his sister.

Gil found a second glass and poured Sadie a glassful of lemonade and a refill for himself.

The drink was cool, tart and sweet at the same time. "Umm. Delicious."

"Used the lemons from our trees here. A new type called Meyer lemons. Brought from China. Almost don't need sugar."

Sadie smiled. "Horticulture a hobby of yours?"

"You might say that. Not an expert or anything." He took a sip and looked off into the distance.

"Some hobbyists know more than experts I've found." She leaned back in her chair. "When did you start working for Dr. Wolf?"

"I met him soon after he married my sister. I was the black sheep of my family. Got myself into some trouble and they washed their hands of me. Hadn't been in touch with them for years. Dr. Wolf didn't know beans about me until I showed up one day out of the blue. Katie was overjoyed to see me, and Asa, he didn't bat an eye. Took me in and sent me to driving school. He believed in second chances. Some people said he liked to keep people beholden, but I never saw it that way."

"Remarkable. Good to hear your take on Dr. Wolf. Not everyone has been so kind."

"Nobody's perfect and that included Asa and also my sister. Katie was pregnant, and it wasn't an easy pregnancy. She was sick most of the time. Dr. Wolf was busy making a name for himself at the hospital. He left early and came home late. And when he was home, he was occupied with his inventions and patents. Katie tried not to complain, but it came out in little ways. She could be sharp when she wanted. The pregnancy and the heat that year didn't help. Asa spent a few nights in the spare bedroom after their spats."

"Must have been difficult."

"They were working through it, looking forward to the new baby. For me, I was happy to have a job and a decent place to stay.

I helped out where ever I could. It was the least I could do. Katie kept saying she was grateful to have me around, not only to help, but someone to talk to.

"Then one day she was dead. She was found in the bath with one of his inventions, some electrical device. Don't know which one, he had a few he was working on.

"For someone who said he wasn't going to talk about his sister, guess I bent your ear some."

"It's okay. I'm glad you got back together with your sister. What can you tell me about Dr. Wolf's charitable activities?"

"Helping me get back on my feet certainly qualifies as a charitable project, wouldn't you agree? What I can tell you is he was just a man. He wasn't perfect. He had faults. Think that applies to everyone, man or woman." He stood. "There's nothing else to tell, Miss Brown. I need to finish up here before the sun sets. Would you like me to show you out?"

"No, I can find my way. Thank you for your time."

Sadie walked out to the street thinking over what Gilbert Shine had shared.

* * *

Gil finished his planting just as the sun set. Then he went upstairs to fix a sandwich. Katie, poor Katie. She deserved better, a better husband, a better brother. At the inquest, he had lied to back up Asa's alibi thinking the man wasn't capable of killing anyone...certainly not his wife and unborn child. He was a doctor, a physician whose life revolved around healing people. But after getting to know the other side of Asa, the dark side, Gil saw things differently. But it didn't matter now. Asa Wolf was dead and sharing space in the Wolf cemetery vault next to Katie and their unborn child.

Unlocking a cabinet over the icebox he removed a bottle of whisky and proceeded to get stinking drunk.

* * *

September 20, 1915

The newspaper office was quiet when Sadie dropped off her weekly column. After the push and excitement of getting the Sunday paper out, there was always a short time on Monday mornings when people felt able to relax for an hour or two.

Her column this week was related to the Sunday visit of former President William Howard Taft. He had spoken at the Expo to a crowd of 7,000 plus people. Numerous reporters had covered the event *ad nauseam.*

Sadie was able to add her own special take to Taft's visit with her column *Flying the Skies*. It was a feel-good column about a ten-year-old polio survivor who had the thrill of his life. He had flown in a Curtiss Trainer over the Organ Pavilion just as the former President walked out to take the microphone.

"Golly! I never saw nothing like it! My friends won't believe it!"

The pilot, an Army Air Lieutenant, was quoted as saying, "It was a pleasure to fly him over the Exposition. He's a great young lad. I expect he'll grow up to be a fine, honorable man." The pilot had read it off a typed card, but Sadie didn't mention the card in the article.

The boy was allowed to sign his name on the eight-foot oak propeller. Roger took a photo of him standing proudly with the use of crutches next to the propeller which towered over the young boy and the Lieutenant.

In the newspaper's basement next to the archives, a mailroom had been shoehorned into a room originally meant for cleaning supplies and storage. It was in a perpetual state of chaos, but the mail seemed to make its way to the correct person eventually.

Employees with little status within the publication and no assigned desk had an inbox 'slot' for mail and notices. A narrow niche had been assigned to Sadie. She smoothed her name typed on a scrap of paper taped under the slot. It looked temporary, but she was confident one day a proper desk would be given to her with her own official inbox. Removing a note from her slot, she read Mr. James in Archives wished to speak with her.

In the Archives, Mr. James hummed *Tip Top Tipperary Mary* as he sorted through stacks of articles. Steam floated up from his cup of tea.

Sadie gave a little knock on the counter. "Don't you just love that song? It's so catchy."

"Good morning, Sadie! Mrs. James would agree with you." He grinned and stood up with a folder.

"After you left the other day, I remembered an article about a clinic in Tijuana called the Wolf Clinic. It's alleged to be a free women's medical clinic catering to the needs of indigent women and children. I wondered if there was any connection to Dr. Wolf. It appears there was. I think you'll find it interesting. Even more so since he managed to have the article pulled before it went to press."

He handed Sadie the article. "If I might recommend, use the typewriter over by the window to copy out what the article says. I keep unpublished articles in a special file drawer, but they have a bad habit of disappearing from time to time."

Sadie sat at the typewriter. Outside the window was a narrow alley. She watched as a man in a buggy pulled close to the building so a Ford delivery truck with construction material could pass. She was sorry to see the passing of the quiet horse and buggy, but not the steaming piles of manure shoveled into piles on street corners by city workers. San Diego got their monies worth from their street cleaners.

The construction material was deposited, and the truck drove off. Tonight, under cover of darkness, workmen planned to dig up a memorial stone and unearth a box next to the flagpole in front of the building. The *Herald's* owner hoped the activity would go unnoticed.

The newspaper's contribution to San Diego's July 4th festivities had been a time capsule buried next to the flagpole and topped with a commemorative stone. Great ceremony had been attached to the dedication of the capsule which was to be opened in 100 years, July 4, 2015. The proud newspaper owner gave every employee a special coin as a souvenir of the momentous event.

Momentous until last week when one of the mailroom boys noticed a package from President Woodrow Wilson which had fallen behind a table. Mailed last June, it contained a portrait and a letter the President wished to have placed in the time capsule. After a tumultuous meeting of minds, it was decided to unearth the box so the portrait and letter could be added. The owner/editor had been quite bad-tempered and fired the mailroom boy (his nephew) in the grand tradition of 'killing the messenger.' After an angry conversation between the owner/editor and his brother, the mailroom boy was reinstated. Sadly, the mailroom continued to remain in a state of disorder.

Checking the ribbon and rolling in a piece of typing paper, Sadie began to type out the article.

>*December 5, 1911 – CHARITY IN OLD MEXICO*
>
>*A certain charitable doctor, who wishes to remain anonymous, is celebrating ten years of operation of a Tijuana clinic that helps indigent and less fortunate women and children. The Clinic called Clínica de Lobos, and its well-known doctor specialize in treatments for female hysteria and other ailments. He takes his copious knowledge to Mexico to help women of all ages and their children. No woman or child has ever been turned away.*
>
>*It is estimated the clinic has helped hundreds, if not thousands, of women and children at little or no cost to the patients. Clínica de Lobos was opened in tribute to the doctor's wife.*
>
>**Source***: Agnes Steves, Agnew Sanitarium aide.*
>**Pulled***: by request of Dr. Asa Wolf*

"Thank you, Mr. James. This might be important." Sadie wondered why Gilbert Shine had neglected to mention the free clinic in Tijuana. It was opened in honor of his sister. Surely he had driven Asa Wolf to the clinic hundreds of times.

"You're welcome, Sadie. I know you have your dream, and I intend to do whatever I can to help. You have the gift of writing, there's no doubt about that. Sometimes our editor can't see talent when it's right in front of his eyes."

* * *

September 20, 1915

Fayette Watkins stared out his office window at the water flying from the sprinkler across the street. The sun made the drops sparkle like tiny crystals. Small birds chattered and crowded around the small puddles of water to drink. The world was full of beauty and at peace.

Except Fayette Watkins felt no peace. He felt gloom deep down to the marrow in his bones. It had been over two months since the Board began their search for a new head of surgery and a new Board member. Waiting for them to find the bald-faced lies in his old employment application was like waiting for water to boil.

Adding to the delay was the detour when they had veered off into investigating Asa Wolf's improper affairs with the nursing staff. That investigation ate up a lot of time, but not one person on the staff would verify the rumors of indiscretion. In the end, the board concluded an ex-employee had concocted the whole sordid story. The gentlemen of the board, all well past their prime, were tired of the inquiry and happy to toss it in the trash. They had gratefully moved on to the initial and easier search for someone to fill the position of head of surgery and a seat around the boardroom table.

A stenographer knocked on the open door of Fayette's office. "Dr. Watkins, sir. The Review Board has asked if you could spare a moment. They're waiting in the boardroom."

Fayette took a deep breath. "Thank you, young man. I'll be right there."

The stenographer was gone in a flash. He had been told to give the message to Dr. Watkins and return immediately to document the coming meeting.

Time ominously slowed to a crawl for Fayette. He took his coat from the hanger on the coatrack and slipped into it. Sweat was forming in his armpits. While the beating of his heart sounded in his ear to be slow and menacing, in reality, it was banging as fast as his Model-T's motor.

The Review Board looked up as he entered the room but didn't rise. The seriousness on their faces did nothing to calm Fayette's feelings of dread. He wasn't invited to take a chair.

The oldest member of the board couldn't have stood if he wanted. A Civil War veteran, he was confined to a wicker and bamboo wheelchair. A plaid blanket covered what was left of his war-damaged legs and conveniently caught most of the ash from his ever-present cigar.

He looked expectantly over his glasses. "Dr. Watkins. Thank you for coming. You are aware, of course, the board has been looking for a replacement for Dr. Asa Wolf as head of surgery."

"Yes, sir." Fayette felt sweat rolling down his sides.

"Sadly, to our distress, we found several discrepancies in the employee files."

Fayette thought about the gold coins and the diamonds in the bookcase secret drawer behind *The Merchant of Venice*. Was there enough to start over in a small town far away from San Diego if he moved tomorrow? He was making calculations when his hearing picked up on the word 'exemplary.'

"I wish all our employees at this hospital had such glowing reviews and comments. Dr. Asa Wolf obviously thought highly of you and your abilities. His research on your education and previous employment helped us immensely with our decision."

The man shifted his body in the wheelchair and straightened the blanket.

"Before we get ahead of ourselves here, are you interested in heading up the department of surgery? It would mean a good-sized raise, but less time in the operating theaters, and involve an abundance of paperwork. Some doctors find it unappealing. How would you feel about the position? Or perhaps you would like a day or two to think over the offer?"

"No, I wouldn't. I mean yes. I mean 'no' I don't need a day or two to think over the offer. And 'yes' I would be extremely interested in heading up the department."

The wheelchair-bound veteran reached out his hand. "Thank you, Doctor. We're quite pleased with your acceptance. I can't rise, but I would like to shake your hand in congratulations."

Fayette smiled and shook his and every other hand offered, including the stenographer's.

"We'll have the legal department prepare the papers and send them to your office for your signature. The wheels of that department run slowly, and it may take a week or two before you receive them. In the meantime, we'll make a formal announcement of your promotion effective today. Also, we intend to recommend to the Board of Directors you be offered Dr. Wolf's seat on the Board. You're young, and we believe the Board could use an infusion of youthful ideas. We'll let you know as soon as we speak with the Board."

Fayette hoped it wasn't unseemly, but he couldn't help but grin with equal parts of relief and celebration.

Fayette walked directly to Asa Wolf's large corner office now empty of boxes. Everything about the office including the view was immensely better than his own. Not only was it larger, it also had a private bathroom and a large closet with a built-in cabinet and enough room for a sleeping cot. For years he had envied Asa this office, now it was his. There was a fleeting second of regret Rose wasn't in his life to enjoy the moment with him, but it was gone almost before it surfaced.

He took a very deep breath and let it out. He had done it. He had gotten away with it, with everything.

CHAPTER 24

September 21, 1915

The murderer finished the perfectly poached eggs and toast, sipped the well-brewed coffee, and sighed with pleasure. The first cup in the morning was always the best. On the table was the morning newspaper opened to page two. At the bottom of the page was a short article.

> ### Police Reopen Missing Person's Case.
> *January 6, 1913, Linda Rush, age 25, was reported missing by her neighbor. Miss Rush, a nurse at a local hospital had left her Boston Terrier with a neighbor while Miss Rush holidayed with friends over the weekend. She promised to return for her Terrier on the evening of Sunday, the 4th. When Miss Rush didn't retrieve her dog as promised, the neighbor went to inquire the following morning. She found Miss Rush's apartment door ajar. Inside was a half-packed suitcase. By all appearances, the apartment was undisturbed. Nothing seemed to be missing except for Linda Rush.*
>
> *Police were unable to determine where or how Miss Rush disappeared. Her family in Chicago and the police are asking for the public's help. If you*

*have any pertinent information, please contact the
San Diego Police Department.*

The murderer took another sip of coffee. It would do no good
to reopen Linda Rush's case. She was past caring and her bones
hidden away where no one would find them. Not one piece of
evidence had been left behind, and there had been no witnesses to
her disappearance. The murderer had been extremely careful
about it.

A clock chimed the hour. The coffee was finished, the
newspaper folded and the murderer rose to start the day.

* * *

September 21, 1915

Insistent doorbell ringing and knocking at the Wolfs' front
door brought Beth running. She wrenched open the door to
discover a pimply-faced delivery boy, clipboard in hand, standing
at the entrance.

Beth started and glared. "Yes? What's all the fuss?"

Forgetting to tip his cap as instructed, the boy grumbled, "In a
hurry. Ain't got all day, ya know. Lot's more deliveries today." He
pushed the clipboard forward. "Sign here."

"Sign? For what?"

"Five boxes from that sanitarium place. Those boxes...heavy
buggers."

"Here! No need for crude language. Take the boxes to the
garage around back. I'll meet you there and sign for them."

The boy's face flushed red. First day on the job and he'd
already screwed-up...just like his ma said he would. Visions of a tip
dribbled away. The way things were these days, any kind of tip
would mean extra food on the table besides beans and potatoes. A
loaf of bread had risen to nine cents! And now he had stuck his
foot in his mouth again.

"Sorry Miss. I'll drive the truck 'round back and unload them
boxes where ever you want 'um."

Beth had the boy put the boxes on a workbench and signed the delivery papers. She grabbed his arm as he turned to go. "Have a hunch this is your first day or close to it. You'll go a lot further if you learn to curtail your rude language."

"I'm sorry, Miss. My ma says I need to think before I say things. I'm trying, but today I missed the trolley to work and near got fired on my first day. Put me in a grouchy place."

"Working for a living isn't always fair. It's not fair a lot of the time. That's a lesson you need to learn early on." She placed a dime and a nickel in his hand.

"Thank you, Miss. Much obliged." He grinned and jumped into his truck. Wouldn't Ma be surprised when he showed her his tip?

The five boxes were tied with twine, numbered, and stamped in large letters on the sides: *AGNEW SANITARIUM & HOSPITAL*. Beth opened the box labeled Number One. Inside, file folders were lined up in precise, alphabetical order. On top was an unsealed envelope addressed to Mrs. Asa Wolf. Lou was visiting her parents, but that presented no problem. Beth often read letters addressed to her employer. Some letters were read with Lou's approval, others were not.

> *Dear Mrs. Asa Wolf:*
>
> *This is to inform you the hospital's legal department has read through all of Dr. Wolf's papers found in his hospital office (contained in the five boxes delivered with this letter) and find nothing of a proprietary nature. It appears Dr. Wolf discontinued his research on the treatment of female hysteria and the use of electricity in 1910. No later research was found. His files contained several patent applications, all of which were rejected and returned by the U.S. Patent Office to Dr. Wolf.*
>
> *If you have any questions, please feel free to contact our office.*
> *Sincerely....*

Beth opened each box searching through the neatly labeled files. In box number five she found the folder she wanted and removed it. Putting the letter and the file folder aside, she took her time and retied each box with the twine. She wrote a note for Gil and left it on top of the boxes.

When Lou returned home after visiting her parents, she found the hospital letter on the hall table. Before changing out of her mourning attire, she read the letter and scowled.

Beth ran a hot bath in which she poured a liberal amount of rose-scented bath salts. She also sat a small silver tray on a table by the tub. "Here's a glass of laudanum topped with cinnamon and a glass of Isolabella."

"Perfect." Water softly sloshed as Lou sank deeper into the tub. Lou sighed, sipped her laudanum, and lit a cigarette. A day spent with her parents was never enjoyable. Add having to dress in mourning and no smoking allowed, it was a day spent in purgatory.

"How was it?"

"The usual. Mother is beyond ridiculous with her pious babble. And she's insisting I should return home to live."

"That sounds frightful."

"Can you imagine? That'll never happen unless I'm on my deathbed."

Beth crossed herself. "Don't tempt fate."

"Where are the boxes from the hospital?"

"In the garage. I left a note for Gil to move them to the shed."

Lou stewed over the hospital's letter. All those nights and Saturdays away doing important research? Liar! Big fat liar! Asa had been a deceiver and a fraud. But was she surprised? Hadn't she known all along? She just didn't want to face it. Now she was forced to accept the cold, hard truth.

She lit another cigarette and reminded herself there was a bright side. How many widows were as happy as she to see the last of their husbands? How many had been left with a tidy bank account? As soon as the insurance paid the money they owed her, her life would be complete.

Lou reached for the tap and added more hot water. When the temperature was to her liking, she eased further down in the tub. Steam billowed and caressed her face like a spa treatment. It was good to be alive.

* * *

September 22, 1915

It was morning, and Beth found Gilbert waxing Asa's Saxon Runabout in the garage. Gilbert was obsessive about the garage. It was always spotless, and each tool had its place. There was even an area set aside to wash and wax the cars.

"Do you have some time to talk, Gil?"

Gilbert clicked the wax container closed and straightened. "Sure, if you don't mind me polishing while you talk. The Saxon needs to look sharp for a buyer coming by today." He checked his watch. "I have to pick up Mrs. Wolf from the bank in thirty minutes, so what's on your mind?"

The driver's door was open on the limo. She sat in the seat and smoothed out her skirt. "I went to the doctor like you suggested."

"What did he say?"

"He says it's not good. Says there's an extreme amount of scar tissue. I asked if he could cut it out, and he said it would make more scar tissue. I wouldn't gain anything. He wanted to know who did it. When I wouldn't say, he called them a butcher." Beth could feel tears welling up.

"I'm probably not the first or the last who had to spend a few days at Lupe's place. Right?"

Gil put down the rag he was using. "That's not something I can answer. You know that. But believe me when I say it's not the end of the world."

"Yes, it is." She jumped out of the limo and leaned into Gilbert's arms and chest. Tears overflowed and burst from her eyes. All the hurt and unfairness she's been dealt came pouring out.

He put an arm around her. "Okay, girl. Get it out."

"No one is going to love me, Gil. Not the way I am."

"Beth, that's not even one little bit true. You're a beautiful young woman. What happened won't make a difference to the right man. I promise you."

"The doctor said the same thing."

"Well, the doctor is right." He pulled her away from his chest. "You'd better stop the waterworks. My uniform is getting wet, and the other one is at the cleaners." He smiled "Besides you look much prettier when your eyes aren't all red. Isn't that what you've said before?"

"Yes. You're right. Besides, it doesn't help to cry over spilled milk. The past is the past. Can't change any of it. I have to remind myself it could have been much worse. If it hadn't been for Maria and Lupe, I might have ended up dead."

"Dead? It doesn't do to think like that, Beth. Here dry your eyes. It's almost time to pick up Mrs. Wolf. You don't want her to see you like this."

"You're right. I'd better get in gear and make up some fresh iced tea for her before you bring her home." She pointed at a fender. "You missed a spot."

Gil laughed. "That's my girl. Back to telling me how to do my job." He rubbed away the missed wax.

"Beth? Believe me. It's going to be all right. The right man will come along when you least expect it."

* * *

September 22, 1915

Buckley opened the door. "Miss Brown. Please come in. Mr. Siebert's at the pool. He's supposed to be swimming laps, but looks to me like he's decided to drink coffee and read the morning *Herald* instead."

"Thank you, Buckley. I'll go around through the garden."

Passing through the side gate, Sadie admired the colors and the scents of the tidy rose garden in full bloom. Roses of all sizes and varieties had been Mrs. Siebert's addition to her son's garden which Elizabeth Siebert viewed as a plain, stark landscape. Sadie made a mental note to speak with Mrs. Siebert. Her engagement party was in the planning stage and groupings of fresh roses would make lovely centerpieces. There was one special rose she liked, white with a touch of pink. They were showy and smelled delicious, just like cinnamon rolls.

The pool area had been designed like Roger's house, all clean lines, and neutral colors. It would have been off-putting and uninviting except for groupings of Adirondack chairs painted in shades of blue and green and a great many large terracotta pots bursting with colorful flowers.

As Buckley described, Roger, a terrycloth pool robe wrapped around his waist and hips, sat on the lip of the pool letting his legs dangle in the water. He was sipping coffee and reading the morning paper.

When he heard footsteps, he turned to see who was invading his morning 'exercise.' "Lovely, Sadie. What a wonderful surprise! Would you like some coffee?"

"Thanks, but no. I came by for your help if you're not booked with photography appointments.'

"No appointments. How can I help?"

"Would you fancy a drive down to Tijuana for a bit of investigating? There's a women's clinic Asa Wolf operated there. Just found out about it. If you'll go with me, I'll treat you to lunch at the Border Grill."

"Investigating? Sounds mysterious and interesting. Always up for mysterious and interesting. And you know me, I can't get enough of Border Grill's handmade tortillas and salsa. When do you want to go?"

"As soon as you're decent."

Roger dressed and the two were on their way south in Sadie's Model T. They tossed a coin to see who would drive. Roger won.

The US & Mexican border guards knew of the clinic and gave them directions.

"Don't expect much. Someone told me it had been broken into and ransacked. Pretty much a mess now I expect."

On a side street in what could be called downtown Tijuana, they found the clinic. A sign, *Clínica de Lobos,* was discreetly painted on a front window. A window that was now caked with reddish-brown dust. Around back, they found a broken windowpane and the door unlocked. Stepping inside, Sadie gasped. The stink of stale urine and rotting food was pungent.

"Worse than I expected. The word 'mess' is an understatement. Looks like vandals went out of their way to trash the place. Sad when you think about it."

"To be expected. The supply of drugs in here would be too much to pass up. Guessing someone got high and went a little crazy."

Someone or ones had broken in and searched for drugs and anything else they could steal, use or sell. Scattered surgical instruments, upended exam tables, an empty, mangled glass and metal cabinet meant to contain drugs all pointed to a thorough and chaotic search of the small clinic. Roaches scurried into cracks as the two moved about the clinic. People had left their names and messages written on the walls.

A dirty padded room used for surgery was littered with trash, cigarette butts, the remains of half-eaten food, and items of a more unpleasant nature. In the corner, grimy pillows and blankets had been piled. A rat glared from under a blanket next to a pile of used syringes and needles.

Roger took a quick look around, felt sick and walked out into what must have been the waiting room. "A surgery with padded walls? Never heard of such a thing, have you?"

The door to Asa's office had been locked, but no longer. "Looks like someone took a hammer to the lock. Not subtle but effective." Inside, desk drawers had been emptied. A file cabinet was open, the papers and folders scattered. They looked through the papers but found nothing of use.

On the desk, an empty bottle of cheap tequila was setting on a book. Water stains and cigarette burns covered its leather cover. Still legible was the gold inscribed name of Dr. A. Wolf. Sadie took the book and opened it. "Looks like a journal. Maybe it holds the answers to some of my questions."

She took hold of Roger's arm. "Let's get out of here. This place makes my skin crawl."

"I agree. It doesn't make sense, but it feels like the padded walls in the surgery room are screaming."

"What? Like ghosts? Since when do you believe in ghosts? This is something new."

"I thought ghosts were hokum until just now. After this, I'll have to re-examine my thoughts on spirits and ghosts. Lord, this place would make anyone think the walls were talking, not to mention fostering nightmares."

* * *

At the Border Grill, Sadie and Roger poured over Asa's journal. It was a gold mine of accounting. In addition, Asa and his nurse had listed names, dates and medical procedures performed by the 'charitable' Dr. Wolf. In the 'treatment' column the word 'expiry' was used regularly followed by 6 wks, 10 wks, 3 mos, etc. Sadie gasped at the fees for an expiry.

The Grill's waitress with red flowers in her jet-black hair placed a basket of hot corn tortillas, chunky red salsa, and steaming bowls of chili verde on their table. Roger spooned salsa on a piping hot tortilla, took a bite and chewed thoughtfully. "So what do you think?"

"What do I think? I think Wolf was spending his Saturdays terminating pregnancies for California girls and charging outrageous fees. That's what I think." Sadie closed the book and sat back. "He used the word 'expiry' instead of 'abortion' or "termination of pregnancy,' but that's what he was doing. You notice the majority of the expiry patients are referred to by initials only. He was covering his rear. The book wouldn't hold up in a courtroom against a half-capable attorney."

Roger sipped his beer. "I saw quite a few girls from a place called Lupe's who came for treatment...Soledad, Isabel, Maria, Sally. Didn't use initials for those ladies. And Lupe had a running account. Paid her bill on the first of the month like clockwork.

Besides a split lip needing stitches or a broken bone needing setting, a lot of silver nitrate and mercury were prescribed."

"I saw that. Aren't those two used as a treatment for venereal disease?"

"Exactly. Just a theory, but I'd guess Wolf started the clinic in Tijuana for the women who worked at Lupe's. Probably lucrative from the start. Women in need of VD treatments and abortions would have a safe place to go. From that beginning, he would have seen the advantage of performing abortions for women from San Diego. Women from families who could afford his fees but not the notoriety of a 'fallen' woman connected to the family name. Word of mouth could have brought in patients from all over."

Sadie nodded. "Who wouldn't think a qualified surgeon would be safer than a backstreet hack with a coat hanger? Besides, one could walk into his clinic without being recognized by an acquaintance strolling past."

Roger opened the book and pointed at a couple of entries. "Look. Some days he performed three or four surgeries. He must have been raking in the money." Roger took another bite of his tortilla.

"Did you read the last entry?"

"The one that said Maria got the bleeding stopped, wrapped up R.R. in blankets, bundled her into the family limo and sent home? Limo? Rich family? That's one surgery that could have gotten him in scalding hot water or worse if the poor gal had come to a bad end."

"Who says it didn't end badly? And if it did? Could a father or a lover think a dead daughter or mistress was a reason for murder?" Sadie had yet to take a bit of food. Her mind was reeling over what they held in their hands.

Roger tucked into his chili verde. "Good point. But there's no written proof of illegal surgeries. It's all supposition on our part. Unless you can find someone willing to speak out about what they saw or experienced, this part of your article is a no-go."

"There might be a way I can include the clinic as a side note in my article. But it would have to be written carefully. I don't propose to be a yellow journalist. And I certainly don't want to be sued for liable by Louise Wolf's lawyers."

CHAPTER 25

September 23, 1915

The Mexican Revolución was going strong, but it didn't seem to scare the thousands of Expo tourists who visited Tijuana, Baja, Mexico. The small town had recently opened what they called a *Typical Mexican Fair in Tijuana, Old Mexico*. Opened July 1st, specifically to appeal to the Expo *turistas*, the Fair delighted the hordes of people who arrived by auto and bus every day to shop for souvenirs and marvel at Mexico's culture.

The colors, music, costumes, food, and dancing captivated them. It was exactly the same colors, music, costumes, food, and dancing at the San Diego Exposition. But somehow it seemed more authentic twenty miles away across the United States/Mexico border.

* * *

Five miles west of Tijuana and overlooking the Pacific Ocean, El Camarón Cantina squatted on the ocean side of a sandy coastal road. Built with reclaimed wood from a shipwreck, the Cantina featured fire-roasted seafood, mouth-burning salsa, beer, and tequila.

Sitting among a profusion of red and purple bougainvillea bushes gone wild, it boasted an attached wooden deck built on pilings over the sand. Patrons could enjoy their Baja shrimp and beer or tequila outside and watch beachcombers search for shells, sea glass, and other treasures. It was a spectacular spot to watch the sun slide into the Pacific each evening.

Precisely at Noon, Simon Bennet sat a table next to the deck's railing. He slowly sipped his Dos Equis and watched sandpipers dash to and fro following the waves. A small boy had built a sandcastle well back from the waterline. He was in the process of decorating it with rocks and shells.

While Simon wished he was throwing back shots of tequila, it would have to wait. Business came first. There had been some bumps in the road, but thanks to Rose Trigby, bless her heart, all eventually worked as planned. She had been surprised and pleased with his first offer of $200. She probably didn't get to spend much of it before her sad accident.

Now, the Drake logbook and map were safely in the hands of the museum and the institution's representative, Ronald Segovia was to meet him here with a check for the agreed $50,000.

A screen door banged, and a man dressed in a cream-colored seersucker suit and holding a Cordova red briefcase stepped from the Cantina. Simon stood with his hand outstretched and smiled. "Mister Segovia. How good to see you again. Please, have a seat. Would you like to join me for lunch? The Cantina's known for its marinated Baja shrimp. Cooked on a wood-burning grill. Delicious."

Ronald Segovia flicked a few specks of dust from a chair with a handkerchief, unbuttoned his coat and sat down. "No, I can't stay. Baja shrimp sounds delightful, but I have another meeting for which I'm already late. So let's skip the formalities and discuss the book." Segovia opened his briefcase and laid the Drake logbook on the table.

Simon swallowed hard. His stomach dropped. "What's this?" he reached for the book, but Segovia pulled it quickly back.

"The museum's antiquities specialist has questions about your historically significant logbook and, might I add, remarkable map. He's a stickler about provenance. According to our 'expert,' this particular logbook was lost during a 1580s burglary and never resurfaced. All documented by the insurance company.

"I, of course, accept your family's story regarding the friendship between your great, great aunt, Sarah, and George Elliot...and that Miss Elliot gave the logbook and map to your aunt as a token of her *friendship*." There was a noticeable emphasis on the word 'friendship.'

"However, nothing is mentioned in George Elliot's papers about the book or her relationship with a Sarah Bennet. So sadly, the museum cannot verify your aunt's story or the provenance. So you see, no authentication."

Simon felt the scam slipping away from his grasp. "I'd be happy to write my parents for a copy of my aunt's estate appraisal done by a reputable appraisal house in New York. Do you think it might satisfy your antiquities specialist?"

"Unfortunately, no. You would think it was the expert's personal money. He's such a little dictator and difficult to deal with." Segovia sighed, and his hand slid towards his briefcase. "However, I have been authorized to offer you a check for $10,000 for the logbook, including the map."

Simon relaxed. The scam was underway again. He had haggled over money before and this was just one more negotiation. He smiled "I feel rather insulted by that amount Mr. Segovia. The agreed-upon price was $50,000. If the museum is still interested in a long-lost Sir Francis Drake logbook and map without provenance, by the museum's standards mind you, perhaps my family would accept $47,000."

Segovia raised a well-groomed eyebrow. He enjoyed a good negotiation. "Maybe I will have lunch after all." He lifted a manicured hand to signal for a waiter. "Tell me, Mr. Bennet, what would your family think of $15,000?"

Simon smiled good-naturedly. He had a feeling that both he and Ronald Segovia were equal masters at the 'game.' He leaned back in his chair and looked forward to an entertaining negotiation...followed by many shots of Tequila.

CHAPTER 26

September 23, 1915

It was a perfect day. A mild, steady Pacific breeze and a cloud-free sky made for ideal flying weather. Riding the ferry from Coronado, Sadie could hear the drone of the aeroplane motors erupting from the newest Curtiss Trainers flying over North Island and south past the Hotel Del Coronado. It was music to Sadie's ears.

Her lessons were confined to the older style pusher aeroplanes. Truth be told, she preferred them. With the engine in the back pushing the craft forward and the pilot sitting up front, she was able to see exactly where she was going. There were no blind spots. And, the strong stench of gasoline fumes stayed behind her. She hoped to purchase a pusher of her own someday.

Like always, the airfield smelled of hot oil and burning fuel. The deafening sounds of engines and men shouting set Sadie's heart pounding. She vibrated with excitement. It was similar to the anticipation of the first day at a new school but so much better.

She and her instructor had another discussion about learning to pull out of a spin, but today wasn't the day to learn how. Important visitors from the Curtiss Company were visiting. "Next time, okay? I promise. I want time to work with you without being distracted."

"I'm holding you to it. You promised, and I won't forget."

He laughed. "I'm sure you won't."

She fastened her goggles and leather hat and stepped up into the open pilot's seat. Her instructor grabbed the propeller and yelled "Contact!" She gave a curt nod and yelled back, "Contact!" Using his body weight, he wrenched the propeller down with the help of a loud grunt.

The engine roared with life shaking the craft and wanting to tear down the runway and into the sky. Sadie could feel it deep inside. She released the brake, the plane leapt forward, and within seconds they sailed into the blue. They were partners. Sadie and her magical Pegasus depending on each other to fly and to stay alive. A blend of wood, cloth, metal, flesh, blood, and bones. The word 'thrilling' came to mind but didn't come close to matching the emotion.

The sun and wind beat against her. Exhilaration cleared her mind like nothing else. No space to think of anything other than this exact moment with her feet and hands on the controls and her eyes on the horizon, the ocean and the sand below, and the beauty that encircled her.

When her airtime was at an end, she dipped her wooden and cloth Pegasus down toward North Island and started her descent back to earth, back to life as a writer and to find a killer.

* * *

Settled on the ground, Sadie sat on a bench and looked at her notes. Putting together an investigative article about Dr. Asa Wolf was not the easiest of stories. She had found plenty of maybes and possibilities, but few facts to substantiate them. There were newspaper stories, medical journal articles, school records, patent records, and unhelpful interviews, all of which proved little if anything.

Unanswered questions abounded about his supposed research, the death of his first wife, and the free clinic in Tijuana. And what about his murder? She refused to call it a natural death.

The list of her verified facts was short.

1. Dr. Asa Wolf was born November 1, 1870, in San Diego to school principal, Bevel Wolf and his wife, Cora Wolf.

2. He graduated from USC Los Angeles medical school. And regardless of Lou Wolf's story, Asa didn't graduate first in his class. Not even close to first. His professors noted he was intelligent but had difficulty listening to and taking orders from authority figures.

3. He unsuccessfully tried to start his own practice and eventually began working at Agnew in 1900. That was the same year he married Katie Shine.

4. Katie and her unborn child died on July 7, 1901. According to her death certificate, it was attributed to accidental electrocution.

5. 1909 he met Louise Watkins, and they married in 1910.

6. May 1915 Wolf advertised in the newspaper wanting to sell a Francis Drake logbook and map. An obvious scam that might have gone terribly wrong.

7. July 8, 1915, Asa was found dead due to a heart attack.

8. Checking the records, Sadie found Wolf had applied for several patents, but all were rejected. His research appeared to have come to a halt after his first wife's death.

9. He had run a secret clinic in Tijuana and performed illegal surgeries, but even with his journal, it probably wouldn't hold up in court.

10. He sometimes drank too much and bragged about new research and new patents, all of which were evidently in his head.

She put a checkmark by number six as something that could use further research. The scam could have led to a disgruntled buyer. Maybe someone angry enough to kill. But the journal seemed to be her best bet.

Pulling Wolf's journal from her folio, she wished it could talk. She had a feeling this was where she'd find the clue telling her who and why Wolf was murdered. Tonight after dinner with Roger and his mother, Sadie planned to finish reading the rest of it.

CHAPTER 27

September 24, 1915

It was early Friday morning, and the city was starting to hum with life. One exception was the San Diego Police Department. It was quiet, normal for a Friday morning. Clerks and officers enjoyed the peace while it lasted, because the evening would soon arrive with the usual Friday-night shenanigans. Between the hodgepodge mix of sailors on shore leave, tourists in town for the Exposition, college students blowing off steam, and the usual drunks, anything could happen and get out of hand. Most issues were easily resolved, but the police could always count on dealing with a few difficult problems. For now, the call board was quiet.

Sergeant Greenway was reading another tiresome noise complaint regarding the Pastime Gun Club in Mission Cliff Gardens. Sadie Brown's arrival was an appreciated interruption. He stood up and motioned to the chair next to his desk. "Miss Brown, please have a seat. Would you like some coffee? It's not the best, but it's hot."

She laughed. "No thanks. Your description is not what I would call enticing. Besides, I'm here to toss around some ideas and suspicions I have regarding Dr. Wolf's death. Or more accurately, Dr. Wolf's murder."

Greenway set the gun club complaint to the side and leaned forward. "I'm all ears, Miss Brown. Tell me what you have."

Sadie had already decided not to reveal her possession of the Wolf Clinic journal. Greenway might want to take the book, and she hadn't finished reading it. Last night she fell asleep before she could turn a page.

"Yesterday I went through all my notes. Over the course of my research, I found some unusual things. They might contribute to your investigation."

"Exactly what I was hoping for."

"First, Dr. Wolf's first wife died in 1901. Were you aware of that or looked into the situation?"

"July 7, 1901. As it happens, I was one of the officers called to the Wolfs' house that day. I was a rooky, and she was my first death. It wasn't a pretty sight. Electricity does terrible things to a body, and she was pregnant besides. I was forced to run outside to vomit. To this day I wonder about Wolf's involvement. He appeared to be in shock and upset, but something didn't sit right with me. Wish I could tell you what bothered me, but think it was more of a gut feeling. You could call it intuition.

"He had an alibi, you know. He was at the hospital. His nurse and his driver verified it. There was nothing further I could do.

"I looked into it again the day Dr. Wolf's body was found at the Lath House. I asked the coroner to take a look at the notes made about Mrs. Wolf's death and tell me what he thought. He concurred with the original opinion of accidental electrocution."

"Were you aware his wife's brother was his driver?"

"No. But it doesn't change the alibi. Maybe the nurse could have been persuaded to back up his alibi, but I doubt his brother-in-law would have done so."

"How about the free clinic in Tijuana he started?"

"So you found Clínica de Lobos. I knew you'd make a good undercover investigator. That clinic is another issue altogether; our hands are tied legally. We're aware he was treating prostitutes and women from San Diego and providing illegal abortions at his so-called "free" clinic. Understandably, a woman wanting an abortion would think a qualified doctor would be better than a quack in a backroom. The whole charity angle was just a front, not his main purpose. It was all about the money."

"That's my thought too."

"However, we couldn't do anything. Not our jurisdiction. We contacted the Tijuana Police. Their response was they'd look into it. If they did, they didn't share their findings with us."

"Was there ever a complaint filed against him here in San Diego?"

"No. Not one unhappy patient or family of a patient ever contacted us. I sent a request to the American Medical Association and to the hospital asking about complaints. Nothing."

"Doesn't make sense. Every doctor, no matter how skilled, must get complaints now and then."

"I agree. But remember he had the money to keep secrets secret. My guess is he paid off disgruntled patients and their families."

Sadie leaned back disappointed. "Guess I'm not much help as a police informant. My research is getting us nowhere. People sidestep my questions and some have flat out stonewalled me. His friends and co-workers at the hospital insist he was a great guy, walked on water, etc. I'm not helping you, and my grand expose is going nowhere.

"The only people who would talk to me with some honesty are the Wolfs' maid, Beth, and Gilbert Shine, the family's driver. But I can tell even they were holding back. Speaking of Mr. Shine, I think I'll pay him another visit. He didn't mention it when I spoke with him, but he must have been driving Wolf to Tijuana."

"Just be careful, Miss Brown. Phrase your questions carefully. This could be a hornet's nest. I don't want you to get stung."

Sadie smiled. "Don't give it a second's thought. I'll tread lightly."

To herself, she added, 'I hope treading lightly will get me what I need. If I can't write a story proving to my editor that Miss Sadie Brown is a top-notch journalist who deserves her own desk at the *Herald*, I may have to tread more on the heavy side.'

* * *

At the corner of 2ⁿᵈ and C streets, Earle C. Anthony's new Packard and Reo Dealership shouted '*Come In Now!*' and '*See What We Have!*' with bunting and signs proclaiming the arrival of the first 1916 models. Simon Bennet ran his hand along the smooth, waxed fender of a new 1916 twin six Packard. The gold pin stripping was immaculate against the black body paint.

Like a man who won against the odds at the Kentucky Derby, Simon was flush with money. After some crafty negotiations, the logbook sold for an excellent price. The museum's check was cashed and split three ways. He felt the money in his pocket warming up. It wasn't exactly burning a hole, but close to it.

He couldn't be happier that Asa, the cheating jackass, could only watch from his place in Hades while he, Ezra, and Jeffrey celebrated and spent every penny. Well, maybe not Ezra. The bean counter probably had the first penny he ever made.

A slick auto salesman rushed to introduce himself and start his spiel.

"Just arrived this morning, Mr. Bennet. Finest automobile built. Packard's Henry Joy drove one just like it clean across the country to the Exposition in San Francisco. Didn't have a bit of trouble. Yep, it's a pip, I'll tell you. We're taking orders if you're interested. You'd be the first order and the first person in San Diego to drive Packard's new twin six. We plan to put a photograph of the first purchaser and his twin six in the window and the newspapers. A fine feather in your cap, Mr. Bennet. Something to make you and the family proud."

Simon checked the price tag again. Almost $5,000. Packard was a great car, no argument there, but pricy. In comparison, the Reo 7-passenger touring car parked next to it was selling for $1,100. With his cut from the logbook scam, he could afford the Packard easily, but touring cars weren't his style. He was a roadster man. Always had been. Always would be. If the salesman had let him get a word in, he would have told him in the beginning.

"I'm not ready for a touring car right now."

"You in the market for a runabout? Packard has a beaut. We have one around back that came in this morning. The lot-boys are detailing it before putting it on the floor." He tilted his head toward the back door. "Come with me, Mr. Bennet. It'll knock your socks off."

The lot-boys were finishing up. The twin six Runabout glistened from the wood spoke wheels to its convertible top.

Simon grinned. "I think I'm in love."

"I thought so." The salesman leaned close and whispered. "Maybe I can get headquarters to sell you this one instead of making you wait."

The needle on Simon's con-meter swung to the far right. "Interesting." He walked around the car again. This time he looked carefully. "Is there a problem?"

The man was smooth as glass, didn't even flush with embarrassment for getting caught out. "A small one which we are taking care of. There's an operational problem with the top. Not a big deal. It takes a couple of extra steps to lower it. The proper parts'll be here within the week. Of course, it won't hinder your driving. We'll call you as soon as the new parts arrive. Our men can replace everything in a whiz-bang."

"I'll get back to you on it." Simon nodded and walked to his flashy red roadster parked on the street.

The salesman nodded back. No matter about Bennet. The signs announcing the arrivals of the 1916 Packards and Reos were drawing people in like flies. He'd already made his quota for the month. He and the misses were making plans to use the extra sales commission for a well-earned vacation up the coast.

On the street, Simon gave his auto a pat. "No worries. You're far sleeker and better looking than the Packard runabout."

With his money clip stuffed with a wad of money, Simon was ready for a celebration. Pretty Lou Wolf came to mind. He wanted to tell her about a potential buyer for the house. In addition, he might get her a little tight and into bed again. At least he would give it the old college try. He smiled, started his little red beauty, and drove off toward the Wolf house.

Gilbert Shine was carrying boxes down to an outbuilding at the back of the property when Sadie arrived.

Sadie plastered on her best and friendliest smile. "Mr. Shine. I hope I'm not bothering you."

"No, just putting some boxes in the shed. Mrs. Wolf and her brother are at the cemetery tending to the family vault and picking out a stain-glass window. Not sure where Beth is. I'll be happy to let them know you called. Any message?"

Sadie decided to get to her questions about the clinic in a roundabout way. "No. Once again, it's you I want to talk with. Just a couple of questions I meant to ask last time we talked."

Gil sat a box down. "Okay, shoot."

"You worked for Dr. Wolf for quite some time. From what you said before, I think you respected the man. But did you know anyone who might want to hurt him or see him murdered?"

"Well, he didn't walk on water. He could rub people the wrong way especially after a couple of drinks under his belt. But I don't personally know of anyone who wanted to see him dead."

Sadie couldn't help but notice the boxes Gil was moving were stamped *AGNEW SANITARIUM & HOSPITAL* on the sides. "Did the legal problem with the hospital and the Wolf estate settle?"

"I believe it did. After all his hard work, I heard Dr. Wolf never got any of his inventions patented. I'm sure the patent office knows what they're doing but just doesn't seem fair. I know he worked like a dog on a number of projects back when he was married to my sister."

"That's a shame." Hoping it would be a good segue, she slipped in her next question. "Was he using his office in Tijuana as a workshop?"

"Oh, the clinic? No, that was a free clinic he started after Katie, my sister, died. He helped a lot of needy women and children down there. I'd drive him down early Saturday morning and he'd work all day. Even though he didn't charge a penny, he told me some women insisted on paying with an egg or two. Can you believe? We all have our pride don't we?"

"I heard he helped people who could pay too."

"The 'working ladies' you mean? Of course he helped them. He never turned anyone away who needed his help. The women and even their madams would come for medical treatment. Those people he charged. They were making money after all. The doctors in Tijuana didn't want to treat them. Their religious upbringing I guess. You know, right and wrong, black and white. That sort of thing. Probably didn't stop them from using the ladies' services when no one was looking. Always the way, isn't it?"

"That's true. Some people talk about religious values and then park them at the curb when they're inconvenient. From what I gather, people in San Diego were unaware of the clinic. Why did he keep it a secret from everyone?"

"Secret? Didn't know it was. Never gave it much thought I suppose. He told me he started the clinic to help him deal with his grief over Katie's death. Asa helping women and children trying to scrape through life with not a dime to their names would have made Katie happy. But keeping it secret? I can't guess about that."

"Wolf stopped a story about the clinic from publication at my paper. Why do you suppose he did that? Was anything illegal happening? There are rumors he performed abortions down there. And not just for the 'working ladies,' but women from the San Diego too."

Gilbert's eyes blinked liked Morse code. He ran his fingers through his hair and looked unnerved. "Where did you hear that?"

"I can't say. They asked me not to use their names."

"They?" He looked at his watch. "It's late. Don't want to be rude, but I have to pick up Mrs. Wolf and her brother in a few minutes. Better get these boxes in the shed. If you wouldn't mind, you can show yourself back out through the gate."

"Maybe we can talk later."

"I think I've told you all I know, Miss Brown. Again, I don't want to be rude, but I have things that need to be done." He picked up two boxes labeled "Number Four" and "Number Five."

As Sadie turned to leave, she saw Beth, Mrs. Wolf's maid, walking through the gate with a bag of groceries.

Beth looked startled, then smiled. "Miss Brown. Trying to lure our driver away from us?"

She laughed. "No just having a chat about Tijuana."

"Oh?" Beth sat the groceries on a table by the stairs leading to Gilbert's apartment. "Gil, I found everything on your list except for the Bay Rum soap. Supposed to get more in next week."

Pushing her hair back, she turned to Sadie. "How about some iced tea, Miss Brown? We can have a heart-to-heart while Gil fetches Mrs. Wolf and Dr. Watkins."

"Sounds nice. Thank you." This was promising. A 'heart-to-heart' sounded as though Beth had something important to share. That would make her trip here worthwhile.

"Have a seat by the pool. It's shady there. I'll bring out a pitcher. Used jasmine green tea from Chinatown. It's Mrs. Wolf's favorite."

Sadie sat in the shade and watched Gilbert carry the last two boxes to the shed. Back in the garage, he fiddled with this and that lever on the Peerless Limo and then gave the crank a hefty turn. It started with a smooth little cough. As he drove down the driveway, he nodded and tipped his chauffeur's hat. Sadie nodded back and opened her notebook. At the street, he turned right towards the cemetery.

The French doors opened and Beth walked out. Behind her, Simon Bennet followed carrying a silver tray with a pitcher of iced tea and glasses.

CHAPTER 28

September 24, 1915

"Hope you don't mind if Mr. Bennet joins us. He was knocking on the door when I went in to fix our iced tea tray. He's going to wait for Mrs. Wolf.

"Mr. Bennet this is Sadie Brown. She works for the *San Diego News-Herald*."

Sadie flipped close her notebook. "Mr. Bennet and I have met before."

"The Women's Press Club's charity auction, right? You were wearing that gorgeous Tiffany bracelet. Diamonds and an amazing sapphire as I recall."

"You have an excellent memory."

"When it comes to beautiful women and diamonds, my memory is perfect."

Simon pulled out a chair. "Beth, my love, have a seat, and let me serve you for once." Simon's smile was warm and seemingly sincere. Sadie couldn't pinpoint why, but it put her on edge. Something about Simon seemed off-putting. It appeared she wasn't the only one. Beth looked uncomfortable too.

He poured the tea into three tall glasses and handed one to Beth and one to Sadie. He lifted his glass in a salute. "Ladies!" He took a tentative sip and then drank more. "Delicious, Beth. One can always tell when people use good quality tea."

"Thank you, Mr. Bennet." Beth sat stiff and unsmiling. Sadie felt an undercurrent of tension but didn't have a clue why.

Mercifully, the Peerless came up the drive. Simon finished his drink and walked over to open the limo door for Lou Wolf. "Lou, you look lovely." It was true. She did look lovely. Mrs. Wolf didn't look like she's spent two grief-stricken hours at the cemetery.

He reached out a hand to Lou's brother to shake. "Fayette, nice to see you too. It's been too long.

"Hope you don't mind me stopping by. Wanted to talk about a business matter. A friend of mine is looking for a good-sized home in San Diego. He lives in Elsinore where it gets hotter than Hades during the summer. Last week he came down to visit the Exposition and fell in love with San Diego and the weather.

"He's a huge fan of Irving Gill, so I drove him by your place. Gill's Dodge House in West Hollywood is a favorite. Wouldn't you know, he thinks your place is similar in all the right places? Perfect for entertaining, he says. He wants to make an offer. Before you ask, he has plenty of the green stuff. Owns a ton of railroad stock."

Lou tucked a stray lock of hair behind her ear. "Interesting. Come inside and let's talk." She looked over at Sadie. "Did we have an appointment I forgot?"

"No. Just having some iced tea with Beth. I hope it doesn't interfere with anything?"

"Not at all." Lou turned to Simon. "Come inside. Fayette and I both need a good stiff drink after two hours at the cemetery. Join us. Then I'd like to hear about this potential buyer for the house. I don't think I'm ready to sell, but if the offer is high enough, I might be persuaded."

Gilbert turned the limo around and drove off on an errand leaving Beth and Sadie alone.

Beth leaned forward. "So Miss Brown, I'm curious. How is the article coming along? The one about Dr. Wolf?"

"Slow going, to be honest. But recently I learned something significant. I read an unpublished newspaper article about a private medical clinic in Tijuana Dr. Wolf was supposedly operating. I came over today to talk with Mr. Shine about it assuming he drove Wolf to Mexico to work there. Didn't get far with my line of questioning though."

"Sometimes it can be difficult to get Gil to say much. He's one of those men who work hard and talk little. So what did the article say?"

"It was about a free women's clinic in Tijuana for women and children. It implied Dr. Asa Wolf was the benefactor but didn't say so directly. I was curious, so a friend and I drove down there. The clinic's pretty much in shambles. But what's truly exciting is I found a journal filled not only with financial information but also Wolf's personal notes. Appears he was performing abortions and making a lot of money at it.

"All my inquiries are pointing to death by foul play. I'm convinced he was murdered, and I'm hopeful the journal contains clues to his murder...the name of his killer and why."

"Murder? Really? Did you mention murder to Gil?"

"I did. He brushed off any suggestion of murder. But he did tell me how the clinic started and the medical treatments Dr. Wolf provided. Praised Wolf to the moon and back. When I asked about abortions, he put a stop to the discussion. He decided he had to finish storing boxes and pick up Mrs. Wolf and Dr. Watkins at the cemetery."

"Tell me more about this journal you found. Sounds fascinating. Did you give it to the police?"

"No, not yet. I want to finish reading it before I hand it over to the police. I'm hoping it's the key to his murder and, not to mention, a great newspaper story."

"How exciting. I love a good mystery. Do you think he might have been blackmailing the women, you know, after the fact? Certainly would make someone want him dead."

"I don't think so. Extorting people takes a lot of time and effort. From what I've gathered, he was too busy with his mistresses to spend time working on blackmail schemes."

"Guess we never truly know people. We all have secrets, right?" Beth cocked her head as though trying to remember something. "Now that you mention a free clinic in Mexico, it seems like I saw a couple of files about a Tijuana office in Wolf's papers.

Agnew just sent them to us, and Gil stored them down in the shed. Maybe there's information in them that would help with your investigation."

"Really? I'd love to see what's in the files."

Beth pointed toward a small outbuilding at the back of the property. "Head down to the shed. I'll fill up our glasses and be right behind you."

Sadie followed the crushed rock path down a slope leading to the building. She didn't want to get too excited, but maybe things were finally coming together. The files might hold the final pieces of the puzzle.

Inside the shed, it was dark and smelled of musty, unwanted furniture, dusty travel trunks, gardening tools, and mothballs. Watery, dim light struggled through a glass-block window. Below it stood a workbench heaped with boxes.

Beth struck a match and lifted the glass chimney on a kerosene lamp. "I'll get this lit and find those files for you. Never wired for electricity in here. The place is full of junk and kind of smelly, sorry.

"You'd think a house as big as the Wolfs' place would have an attic, but it doesn't. Mrs. Wolf had the shed built right after we moved in, kind of combination garden shed and storage. No electricity but there's a sink with running water which is nice after digging in the dirt or rummaging through dusty boxes." She handed Sadie a rag. "Dust off a chair and have a seat. Relax and drink your tea before the ice melts."

"Can I help?"

"No, thanks. I've got it. Shouldn't take but a minute or two."

Sadie sipped her drink and pictured the look on her editor's face when he read her expose about the great Dr. Asa Wolf and his illegal surgeries, the strange death of his pregnant wife and his mysterious demise. She let her eyes close a tiny bit. Her breathing slowed.

CHAPTER 29

September 24, 1915

When Sadie awoke it was pitch black. For a fragment of a second she panicked, but straightaway the logical thinking she'd inherited from her father took over. O&A. She wasn't able to observe, but she could assess. She couldn't see, but she could hear. And what she heard was not good...the slow drip of water and heavy breathing. She tried to move, but couldn't.

Beth took a deep breath and let it out slowly. "Don't struggle Miss Brown. I've tied you quite well to the chair. You're blindfolded and gaged. But, if you promise not to scream, I'll remove the gag. Screaming won't do a bit of good anyway. We're too far away from the house and the garage for anyone to hear. Nod if you're going to cooperate."

Sadie nodded. Beth removed the gag. "No reason for the blindfold either I suppose."

Sadie blinked at the sudden light and licked her lips. Her mouth felt like she'd been eating moldy bread.

Beth held a glass of water to Sadie's lips. "Drink this. The stuff I spiked your drink with gives you horrid dry mouth."

Gratefully drinking the water, Sadie thought the only thing worse than what was happening here would be piloting an aeroplane and having the engine quit. Or moving back in with her grandparents. Oh yeah, that would be bad.

Unexpectedly, Sadie heard her father's deep voice clearly. *"Sadie. Forget your aeroplane and your grandparents. Observe and analyze the way I taught you."*

Beth was moving boxes and gardening tools around on the table.

"Guess you're wondering what's going on, huh? Miss Brown? Miss meddlesome?"

Sadie cleared her throat. Even after the water, her mouth felt dry as sand. She swallowed and tried testing the ropes tying her to the chair. "Want to tell me what this is about? Why am I tied up?"

Beth turned to face her captive. "My, aren't we the unshakable one. Most people would be terrified and peeing themselves right now."

"To be honest, my curiosity seems to be taking over."

"Must be the reporter in you." Beth turned leaned back against the table. "The reporter that's creating a big problem. Here I thought I was completely safe because everyone wanted to protect Dr. Asa Wolf's memory. But you finding his journal changes things. After reading it, it wouldn't have taken you long to put two and two together and realize Wolf was murdered and who the killer was."

Sadie said nothing, but it was now clear Beth knew more than she had let on. Either Beth killed Wolf or she knew who did. Sadie had a feeling she was about to find out who the killer was and how and why Wolf died.

"What an unbelievable mess. My clever plans have gone to Hell in a handbasket. Lord, I need to think. I need a new plan."

She walked to a trunk in the corner, opened it and peered inside. Then she turned to Sadie and glared at her.

"You probably think I belong in a mental ward, locked up in a padded room after drugging you and tying you up and everything? Well, I'm no monster. I'm not insane. Things just got out of hand, and I'm not sure what to do next. But I know for darn sure I don't want to end up at the end of a rope."

Sadie had her answer. The murderer was in the shed glaring at her.

"But first and foremost, I need the journal!"

"Beth, listen okay? Let's talk this through. I know we can figure things out between the two of us."

"What? You think I'm stupid? You have no idea what you're talking about, okay?"

"Talking things through is great for solving problems, even big ones like this."

"Oh Lord, I'm not an idiot. I should have kept you gagged."

Sadie licked her lips. "May I have some more water?" Beth put the glass to her lips and let her drink.

"Beth why don't you tell me what happened. I'm positive I can figure a way to explain this to the police...like self-defense or an accident. Both good ways to go. No jail time for either of them."

"Kill Wolf in self-defense and then pose his body afterward? Don't think that'll fly. And what about Rose Trigby?"

"Rose? The coroner ruled it as an accident. She slipped while lighting the stove and hit her head on the edge of the kitchen table."

Beth's eyes opened wide. "You don't say? I hadn't heard that."

Geeze, was Beth a serial killer? "Why don't you tell me what happened. Okay? Between the two of us, we can figure a way out of this."

"The police aren't looking into Rose's death?"

"No. It was declared an accident, pure and simple. Case closed. What do you know about it?"

"Well, I'm in deep already. Another foot or two won't make it any worse. It started when Rose showed up unannounced."

"When was that?"

"A few days before I...Rose died. She came by the house in her uniform and stood on the street. Just stood there and stared at the house. Didn't take a genius to figure out what she wanted. I sent her on her way before Lou noticed or the neighbors started wondering."

Rose walked back to the worktable.

"So I did what I've always done since the day Lou's mother turned me into Lou's fulltime companion and playmate. I protected Lou from the realities of life. That's what I do. I'm more than a maid you see.

"Very early the following Sunday morning I visited Rose. I knocked on her door. She answered with a big smile. Probably thought I was her newest man making an early morning call."

Beth laughed as she remembered. "She was surprised when she saw me. But after I apologized for the early hour and told her I had a message regarding money from Asa's estate, she invited me in for coffee.

"We went into the kitchen. She was happy as a clam getting coffee and sugar from her Hoosier cabinet, babbling about a fur coat she had to give away. When she picked up a box of matches to light the stove, I gave her the bad news. Told her there was no money. Not one red cent. That knocked the wind out of her sails. You should have seen her face. I made it clear that if she tried to contact Mrs. Wolf again, I'd make sure she'd regret it. I didn't go into detail, but I told her I had already made a couple of Wolf's floozies disappear."

"Goodness, when was that?"

"Never mind about those deluded hussies. It's not relevant to my story."

Sadie's mind went into auto-writing mode...detailing the life of a female serial killer from the killer's point of view. Something a magazine like *Life* or *Collier's* would snap up. Then reality gave her a swift kick. Idiot! She was tied to a chair and may not live to see her beloved Underwood again...or Roger. What would Roger do if she was killed or disappeared? Probably be really sad for a few months and then decide to move on and...

'*Sadie! Get! A! Grip!*' Her father again. Sadie was a bit unnerved by the heated tone of her father's voice, but then she hadn't gotten herself into such hot water before.

Right. Okay. She could and would talk her way out of this.

"So what did Rose say?"

"The woman had no shame. She called me a bitch, shoved me, and laughed when I landed on my butt. I grabbed her ankle and yanked. She fell against the table and was knocked out. So I left."

"I can see how that could happen." Sadie decided not to mention Beth had left out a crucial detail. Someone had turned on the gas, and it hadn't been Rose. "Good you didn't get hurt yourself."

"True. It could have gotten ugly."

"So tell me about you and Asa Wolf."

"Me and Asa? Well first off, he deserved what he got. Okay? I fended Wolf off since the day he met Lou.

"Other than Asa, life was fine until I fell in love with a fast-talker. Before I knew it, he got me in bed, and I was pregnant. I was thrilled. He wasn't. He called me a tramp and accused me of sleeping around. Told me to get lost and then left town. Typical, right?

"So I swallowed my pride and went to Wolf to ask about 'fixing' my situation. For once, he was actually understanding. Said he'd do the termination, and only he and Gil would know. Looking back, he probably wanted something to hold over my head. He liked doing special favors for people to keep them indebted.

"Gil drove us down to the clinic early on a Saturday. Wolf took care of all his paying patients first, nipping on his bourbon as the day wore on. I was the last operation. By that time, I had changed my mind. I wasn't about to let a drunk surgeon near me. Didn't want him to touch me. I just wanted to go home. He laughed and plopped a mask of ether on my face.

"When I woke up the nurse, Maria, was panicking. Her accent was heavy, but she was saying something about blood, lots of blood. I was woozy, so she and Gil bundled me up in a blanket and drove me to Lupe's place to recover. Right. Recover in a whorehouse."

"I'm so sorry Beth. I can't even imagine."

"Wolf messed up the surgery, you know? I have so much scar tissue, no man will ever want me."

"Oh Beth, how awful for you." Sadie was surprised at her feeling of sympathy for the woman in front of her, serial killer or no.

"After I healed, I tried to talk to Wolf about what he did. He threatened me. Told me to keep my mouth shut or he'd shut it for good. Even said he'd tell Lou's parents my mother was stealing from them and get her fired. God, I hated the man."

Beth picked up a pronged gardening tool and scraped it along the worktable. It made angry, deep lines in the wood.

"That was in January. In February I found the perfect solution. But I had to wait a few months. Let him think I was over my mad. Like that would ever happen.

"I make cold curried squid once a year for New Year's Day. It's supposed to bring good luck. Asa loved it when I made it mouth-numbingly spicy. He had a thing for insanely hot spicy food.

The day I killed him, I put a note in his pocket before he left the house. *Meet me in the Lath House tonight after your buddies go home. I have a surprise for you. Beth and your favorite curried squid.*'

"It was the cook's day off. I made the squid and put it in the icebox. After Lou went to bed, I topped the squid with dried fish flakes and chopped extra hot jalapenos and took the trolley to Balboa Park. He was waiting in the Lath House, big grin and all.

"Per usual, the squid was gobbled down. Only I had added an extra ingredient to the fish flakes, dried pufferfish. It's toxic. Causes paralysis. Anything bigger than a pinch can kill a horse."

"Where did you find pufferfish?"

"Chinatown in Los Angeles. A tea and herb shop had pufferfish flakes on a back shelf. The saleslady assured me the flakes would be deadly for rats or whatever else I wanted to kill. As I said, it doesn't take much." She rubbed her jaw and neck remembering.

"Unbelievable, Wolf actually thought I had a change of heart and was going to feed him and then stroke and pleasure his 'ego' there among the banana trees. I managed to keep my cool until he finished eating. Then I kind of lost it and started yelling about the surgery. Don't know what got into to me, but I slapped him. You should have seen the look on his face. Pure rage. He punched me hard enough I lost a tooth. Had a bruise too. Thank goodness for rice powder.

"He screamed at me. Told me I was fired. Told me to pack my things and get out of his house. I started to panic. The toxin wasn't working. No paralysis, no nothing. Then, mercifully, his eyes got big as silver dollars, and he collapsed under a giant fern tree.

"It took some work, but I got him posed. I didn't want Lou to see him looking like he was, all wide-eyed with his arms and legs bent at strange angles. That's me always protecting Lou from real life." She laughed. "Jokes on me because Lou didn't see him until after the funeral home fixed him up." She laughed again.

"But it was thoughtful of you."

"Yeah. But if she hears what I'm telling you, she won't think so."

The last comment sounded ominous. Sadie tried the ropes on her wrists again. "I can see how you'd feel that way. But so far no one knows you were at the Lath House that night."

"Correction...you know."

If Sadie couldn't fast-talk her way out of this shed, she knew a fiancé and a police officer who would never forgive her. But there was hope yet.

"Look, Beth. I think the guy was a complete shit and got what was coming to him. I only want to write a story about his work and his death by heart attack. There's no need to mention murder."

"You expect me to believe you won't go to the police and spill what I told you? You'll have your typewriter out and write a scandalous piece of yellow journalism before the sun goes down."

"Yes. You should believe me. You stopped him from hurting other women. I think that deserves a medal, not punishment." Maybe 'deserved a medal' went too far.

"You'd say that wouldn't you?" She stood by the window and jabbed the garden tool in the wood. "I have to think, okay? It's been a chore to think straight these last few weeks since you began snooping around."

"Beth, you could get away, far away, where no one would know anything about you, change your name and all. Leave me tied up. They'll look in here when they start searching for you."

"And then what? You'd write some front-page article about what I did and become a famous reporter? And me, I'd become an infamous murderer on the run? Is that what you think?"

"No. I'm only trying to help."

Beth grabbed a rag and stuffed it in Sadie's mouth. "Hush up! I need to think. Your jabbering isn't helping."

Beth's mind was racing. She could put more knockout drops in Sadie's water, force her to drink it, untie her, knock over the lamp, and let the shed go up in flames. Would people believe Sadie was rummaging around in a dark shed, trying to light a lamp and accidentally start a fire?

She removed the gag and put the glass of water to Sadie's lips. "Have some more water."

"No thanks. I'm fine."

"Come on. You'll feel better. I promise. I know your mouth tastes horrible."

Sadie took a sip and spat it out. "What did you put in that?"

"Just drink, okay? It's not fatal. It'll only make you sleepy. I'll be long gone before you wake up. I don't want to hurt you. You're a good egg. A nosey egg but a good one."

Saying thank you was a bit much, but Sadie managed a weak smile. The killer standing in front of her with the glass of spiked water smiled back.

"When they find you, you have my permission to write every bit of what I told you. Do me one favor though. Tell Lou I love her more than anything in the world. Would you do that? I don't think she realizes how much she means to me."

CHAPTER 30

September 24, 1915

Beth was pleased as punch. Miss Brown fell for her little speech, and the fire in the shed was taking hold nicely. Turning towards the house, Beth started up the slope. That's when she saw four men racing down the hill towards her and the outbuilding, which was billowing black smoke. Lou was close behind them.

Not fair. Nothing was working right, Beth thought. "Fire!" she screamed. "Fire!"

As they got closer, Beth yelled. "I smelled smoke, and then I saw the shed was on fire. Dr. Wolf's papers are inside. I tried to get them out, but it was too hot."

Sergeant Greenway grabbed Beth by the arms. "Have you seen Miss Brown? She told me she was coming here."

Beth avoided eye contact but forced herself to whisper, "Yes, but I think she left. Maybe. I don't know."

Greenway was getting a gut feeling that horrified him.

He and Officer Henderson ran to the door of the shed. Greenway shouted, "Anyone in there? Hello?" Gil grabbed a hose, opened the water faucet outside the door and started to spray water inside and over the roof.

Greenway stepped inside but the smoke drove him back. He yelled, "Sadie are you in there? Sadie? Yell. Scream. Do something, Goddamit!"

The fire was crackling and the water made it sizzle, but above the noise Greenway heard a moan.

Sadie managed a muffled, "Help." The smoke was making it painful to breathe and impossible to see. She'd lost all direction. Which way was the door? Blindly crawling, her lungs gasping for oxygen, unable to see, and barely able to think, she collapsed just feet from the exit. Giving up is not an option she told herself and forced herself to her hands and knees. In the distance, she could hear sirens. But maybe it was wishful thinking or she was hallucinating.

Probably hallucinating because she also thought she heard her father's panicked voice screaming, "*Keep going! Keep going!*" But that was impossible. He was dead. Then she lost consciousness.

CHAPTER 31

September 25, 1915

When she next opened her eyes, she was in a hospital room surrounded by people. Her throat and chest hurt, and breathing was agony.

Roger was holding her hand. "Don't try to talk. The doctor says you inhaled a lot of smoke, and your eyebrows were singed. But you'll be up and about in no time. For now, you're confined to bed."

Sadie tried to sit up and found she was too weak. But she was awake which meant she was alive. She had dreamt the worst nightmare of her life. Someone had been trying to kill her. Her mind cleared a little more, and she realized someone had indeed been trying to kill her.

"Sergeant Greenway rescued you. After you left his office to talk with the Wolf family's driver, he remembered reading in the file one of Wolf's Phrenology friends said Wolf kept reading a note about a 'surprise from home.' Greenway had one of his gut feelings, and he couldn't shake it. So he and Henderson rode out to the Wolfs' house. They saw the smoke from the street.

"The two of them, Wolfs' driver and that Simon guy raced to the shed to put out the flames. At first, they didn't think anyone was inside. Lucky for you Greenway still had his gut feeling. He kept yelling your name and finally heard moaning. He ran in and pulled you out. By the time the fire brigade arrived, the shed had burnt to the ground.

"You're going to need a few days of hospital rest. Doctor's orders."

A few days of rest sounded wonderful. She hadn't felt such exhaustion before.

"Take a look at all the flowers. No surprise, the roses are from my mother. The big bunch of sunflowers, and I don't know what all, are from the *Herald*. And you thought they barely knew you existed. The purple and lavender ones are from me."

Roger furtively wiped away tears of relief. Almost losing Sadie had been petrifying. Holding her hand and looking at her beautiful face was the most important thing in his world.

"There was an apple pie from Mr. & Mrs. James from the *Herald*. Since you aren't allowed anything except cool broth right now, the nurses and I took care of the pie for you. Think the doctor managed to get a piece too. Delicious. Maybe you could ask Mrs. James for her recipe when you're back on your feet?"

Sadie managed to croak, "Beth?" It hurt like the dickens to speak, but she needed to know.

"Are you trying to ask about Beth? Let's talk about it after you're feeling better. Greenway is pretty keen to talk to you. He'll explain."

He gripped her hand tighter, kissed her cheek and where her eyebrows used to be. "The doc says your eyebrows will grow back as good as new."

Sadie had exhausted the little strength she had and felt herself slipping back to sleep. Roger was still talking, but nothing made sense. Sadie had a million questions but no voice or the energy to ask.

Darkness engulfed her and she was back in dreamland in which Shakespearean witches cackled around a fire tossing bits and pieces of offal in a black pot full of nightmares. Overhead stars danced.

* * *

The following day, Sadie woke up in the hospital to a stern-faced Sergeant Greenway. "I thought we had an agreement between you and me? You were to ask questions but not put yourself in any dangerous situations. So what, may I ask, were you doing in the shed? How did the fire start? Was Mrs. Wolf's maid with you? Did she take you down there?" He put his palm up. "First, Doctor's orders, no talking. But writing is okay so long as you don't overtire yourself. The nurse is going to help you sit up and give you a pad and pencil."

Sadie wrote a few words and showed it to Greenway. *"Sorry. I was a complete idiot. And thank you for arriving when you did and pulling me out of the fire. I'd be dead if it hadn't been for you."*

"You are welcome. And yes, I have to agree, you were an idiot. You scared the heck out of me."

She rubbed her throat.

"More water?"

She nodded and took the glass. The water hurt going down her throat but felt wonderful in her mouth and stomach. The nurse handed her a cup of cool bland, unseasoned beef broth, waited for her to drain the cup and left.

"You feel up to answering some questions?"

She nodded.

"First, briefly, what happened in the shed?"

Sadie began writing and handed Greenway a page with the facts about how Beth had tried to kill her, thinking Sadie was close to figuring out Beth had murdered Asa Wolf and Rose Trigby.

"Well, this shines some light on things. The shed went up like an inferno. There wasn't much left by the time the fire department arrived. And when they looked for what started the fire, they found two bodies. Actually what was left of two bodies. The coroner has them in the morgue, and he's going over them. We think one is Beth. The other one is a mystery. Looks to be old bones. Female, the coroner thinks.

"It's presumed the other was Beth, because while I was pulling you out, she rushed back into the shed. I tried to grab her, but she was too fast. Death by fire isn't a pleasant way to go."

Greenwood awkwardly patted Sadie's hand.

"I'm just relieved you're okay."

The nurse cleared her throat.

"Your nurse is giving me the 'time-to-get-lost' look. But we'll talk again when you're feeling better."

* * *

When Sadie returned home under the care of a nurse in-training who conveniently lived in Sadie's apartment building, Sergeant Greenway stopped by to bring her up to date.

"As we suspected, the abortion clinic Wolf was running in Tijuana was bringing in a ton of money. Agnew had their suspicions about the illegal goings-on at the clinic. It was a big part of the reason they were going through Wolf's papers in his office. They didn't want any association with the clinic to come back and bite them in the behind.

"Beth Hellberg, God rest her soul, put an end to his illegal surgeries."

Sadie felt a deep sadness. Her throat was raw, but she managed to whisper, "I doubt that will be the end of backdoor abortions. Someone else will step up to fill the void. Probably have already."

"I wouldn't doubt it. However, thanks to your help, we now know what happened in the Lath House the night of July 7th."

Greenway ran his fingers through his hair. "Too bad Beth felt the need to rush back into the shed instead of having her day in court. With a good defense lawyer and a sympathetic jury, she might have gotten away with it."

"I tried to tell her the same thing, but she wouldn't listen. More than the gallows, Beth seemed to be terrified Lou would find out she was a killer and end their relationship. Between you and me, I think she was in love with Louise Wolf, although I doubt Mrs. Wolf was aware."

"Interesting. Just goes to show you never know about people. Some live in a fantasy land others can't begin to imagine."

"Beth said something similar about not knowing people. She also said we all have secrets. And speaking of secrets. The other body in the shed? I have a theory about that one." She rubbed her throat.

"Later, okay? You look like you could use a nap. We'll get together again soon. But, I want to take Wolf's journal with me. Like to use what's in it for my report."

She stifled a yawn. "May I have Roger drop it off tomorrow after I type up my article? I want to use it to double-check some facts."

"Okay, but don't forget."

"Promise, I won't. Before you go, if I haven't said it enough, let me say it again, 'Thank you for saving my life.' I'd be dead if you hadn't pulled me out of that shed though the flames and all."

"No thanks needed. Couldn't let my unofficial informant die, now could I? Weird thing. When I heard you moaning and your call for help, it sounded like a man was shouting out too. Strange how your mind plays tricks, huh?"

Greenway looked at the young woman whose fierce determination to be a reporter broke open a case he hadn't been able to crack. "Besides, dragging you from a burning building turns out to have a side benefit. My wife's been cooking my favorite dishes, giving me the comic section from the paper first and other special treats I won't detail. She thinks I'm a hero." He grinned.

"If it hadn't been for you, Wolf's death would still be a question mark. I'd still be losing sleep trying to figure out what really happened. On the other hand, I can't decide whether to be happy or guilty for suggesting you poke around for information."

"Happy, please. Can't wait to help again."

"Well, we'll discuss that later when you're back to your old self."

He nodded his head toward Sadie's desk. "I see your typewriter is setup with a stack of paper beside it."

"Yes. Tomorrow morning I plan to type my expose about Dr. Asa Wolf's strange life of healing, greed and his murder. It's already written in my head. Just need to put it on paper. My editor is waiting to publish it in Sunday's paper."

"Can't wait to read it, Miss Brown."

CHAPTER 32

October 3, 1915

A joyful, multi-purpose celebration was taking place on Elizabeth Siebert's patio. Champagne, food, and floral decorations, mostly white and pink roses, were in abundance.

Roger's mother had never entertained such a mix of people from so many different walks of life. It was exhilarating. Ladies from the Women's Press Club, people from the *Herald*, representatives from the police department, charity shop clerks, aviators from a flying school, and Sadie's grandparents who kept adjusting Sadie's hat. It was wonderful. She smiled and 'mingled' enjoying herself immensely.

Her son, Roger, tapped on his glass for attention. "Everyone! May I make a toast to my lovely fiancé and her newest piece of jewelry?"

There was a gasp of surprise from the people who weren't aware of the engagement. He put an arm around Sadie's waist. She pulled off her glove and displayed an elegant cushion-cut diamond ring. The sun caught it just right, and it sparkled to the heavens and back. A round of happy applause and surprised laughter bubbled from the crowd.

"Can you believe she said yes? I'm the luckiest man in San Diego. But, equally important, we're here to celebrate the birth of a new investigative reporter. It's something Sadie has worked hard for, not to mention almost gave her all.

"For those of you who didn't read this morning's paper, Sadie's investigative article regarding the mysterious life and murder of Dr. Asa Wolf was printed on the *Herald's* front page, and above-the-fold, which I'm told is quite important. I have copies on hand for anyone who hasn't read it...and extras set aside for our grandchildren." He laughed and squeezed Sadie with one arm. With the other, he raised his glass. "To Sadie Brown, *San Diego News-Herald's* newest investigative reporter."

Family and friends raised their glasses and shouted, "Here! Here!" They drank their Champagne, offered congratulations, and dug into the buffet which included Mr. Hiro Ito's prime-rib finger sandwiches, Isaac Buckley's shrimp salad, and Lucinda James' award-winning apple-raisin-walnut with chocolate-drizzle pie.

The End

49 CAMP..... *Part of the Isthmus Fun Zone, Balboa Park. Featured dancing girls and gaming. Closed because of illegal gaming for a short while, but eventually reopened minus the wagering.*

Agnew Sanitarium & Hospital.....*Fifth and Beech, San Diego – five-story brick building with all the latest medical equipment available in 1915. The building no longer exists.*

American Film Company (aka Flying A Studios).....*Silent film company located in Chicago with a unit in La Mesa, California. The La Mesa unit later moved to Santa Barbara in 1912. The company dissolved in the early 1920s.*

Anthony, Earle C. Packard & Reo Dealership.... *Corner of 2nd and C Streets, San Diego. Well known Packard dealership. Originally started in Los Angeles and opened a San Diego showroom in 1915. No longer exists in San Diego.*

Balboa Park.....*San Diego, 1,200 acre site of well-preserved and still in use buildings built for the 1915/1916 Panama-California Exposition. The park contains Museums, gardens, restaurants, several theaters, an organ pavilion, a Japanese Friendship Garden, the San Diego Zoo, a Naval Medical Center/Hospital and much more.*

Bayer's Cocaine Pills.....*The 1914 Harrison Narcotics Tax Act put an end to Bayer's sales of cocaine pills and cough syrup (which Bayer touted as non-addictive) in the US. The ban and tax act began to be enforced mid to late 1915.*

Beverly Hills Hotel.....*Beverly Hills, California. Famed hotel was established in 1912 and is still going strong.*

Blue Mouse Café & Cabaret.....*Coronado, California. No longer exists.*

Border Grill.....*Product of the author's imagination.*

China Wall Café.....*Product of the author's imagination.*

Clinica de Lobos, Tijuana.....*Product of the author's imagination.*

Coronado.....*a resort city across the bay from San Diego.*

Coronado Yacht Club.....*Coronado. Established 1913 and still in existence.*

DAR Tea Room.....*Expo exhibit sponsored by the Daughters of the Revolution.*

Dodge House.....*The Walter L. Dodge House was an Irving Gill designed home located in West Hollywood. Construction started in 1914 and completed in 1916. One of the places where dates were fudged for my novel. Sadly, after attempts to preserve the home, it was demolished in 1970 to make way for apartments.*

Duncan's Bar.....*Product of the author's imagination.*

El Camarón Cantina, Baja, Mexico.....*Product of the author's imagination.*

Fallbrook.....*Small agricultural town 55 miles northeast of San Diego. Now known for their avocado production, but in 1915 the town was a large producer of olives, olive oil, lemons and honey.*

Glenn Curtiss Flying School..... *North Island, San Diego County. Closed in 1916/1917. Some have written that the Curtiss' North Island School closed in 1914 after North Island was taken over by the Army and Naval flight schools. However that seems to be incorrect. Checking the 1915 and 1916 "San Diego City and County Directories" you can find listings for students, instructors, mechanics and other employees working at the Glenn Curtiss Flying School. In the 1917 Directory, there are no listings for the school.*

Goldman's Fine Books.....*Product of the author's imagination.*

Harvey, Fred Lunchroom.....*Santa Fe Train Station, San Diego. The part of the building housing the lunchroom was demolished to make way for parking.*

Hawaiian Village..... *Part of the Isthmus Fun Zone, Balboa Park.*

Holcomb's Department Store.....*Product of the author's imagination.*

Hotel Del Coronado.....*Coronado, 400-plus-room high Victorian hotel. It's still thriving as a first-class, tourist destination hotel. Location for filming Hollywood movies such as "Some Like it Hot."*

Hotel Ellis.....*Fallbrook, California, A hotel built in 1881 and demolished in 1958. A parking lot covers the grounds where it once stood.*

Hotel Redondo (1890-1925*).....Redondo Beach, California. Beautiful 225-room hotel which was condemned and demolished in 1925.*

Isthmus.....*Balboa Park, San Diego. The fun zone at the Exposition – The area it occupied is now a parking lot and a road separating the Expo buildings from the San Diego Zoo.*

Julian.....*a small town east of San Diego and still known for its apple production.*

Lath House, aka Botany Exhibit Building, aka Botanical Building.....*Balboa Park, San Diego. Still part of Balboa Park and a delight to stroll through all the tropical plants.*

La Mesa.....*a small town east of San Diego where numerous silent film companies located early in the 1900s. They later moved on to Hollywood, Santa Barbara and other locations.*

Lee Chang's Aloe & Opium Lotion.....*Such products did exist, but this one is from the author's imagination.*

Lee Sing Import/Export.....*Product of author's imagination.*

Ostrich Farm..... *Part of the Isthmus Fun Zone, Balboa Park.*

Marston's Department Store.....*Original store opened in 1878. A new store was constructed in 1912, an elegant, six-story department store located on Sixth Street in 1915. Sold to The Broadway in 1961.*

North Island.....*across the bay from San Diego. Now home to the Naval Air Station.*

Panama-California Exposition, San Diego (1915-1916).....*Balboa Park, San Diego. Planned as a one-year fair in honor of the completion of the Panama Canal, it continued operating through 1916.*

Panama Film Company..... *Part of the Isthmus Fun Zone, Balboa Park.*

Panama-International Exposition, San Francisco (1915-1915).....*San Francisco. Much larger and profitable fair, it stopped operations at the end of 1915.*

Paris Garden Review, NYC.....*Product of the author's imagination.*

Pastime Gun Club.....*San Diego. The club's trap shooting ranges were located at Balboa Park, Old Town and Mission Cliff Gardens. The range at the Park was closed in 1904 and the other ranges were closed by 1919.*

San Diego News-Herald.....*Product of author's imagination.*

Shaffer's Furniture.....*Product of author's imagination.*

Spreckels Theater, the Electric Trolley System and the Organ Pavilion.....*All operating during 1915 and still active today.*

Sultan's Harem Dancing Girls..... *Part of the Isthmus Fun Zone, Balboa Park.*

Tijuana Mexican Fair.....*Tijuana, Baja, Mexico. Fair opened July 1, 1915 and closed Dec 31, 1915.*

Tokio Café Chop Suey Parlor..... *Part of the Isthmus Fun Zone, Balboa Park.*

US Grant Hotel.....326 Broadway, San Diego. 437-room luxury hotel. Still in operation.

Weiss Hungarian Restaurant.....*Coronado. No longer exists.*

Women's Press Club.....*Product of the author's imagination although there was a San Diego Women's Press Club in 1915.*

Winter Garden Building, NYC.....*Originally built in 1896 as a horse exchange on Broadway. In 1911 it was converted to a theater. It's still standing and providing theatergoers with first-class productions.*

Wong Sing Club.....*Product of the author's imagination.*

INDEX OF PEOPLE
Real and Imaginary

Sunday, Billy (1862-1935).....*former baseball athlete and influential Evangelist.*
Watkins, Gen. Lafayette.....*Product of author's imagination.*
Wong, Danny.....*Product of the author's imagination.*
Yokoyama Taikan (1868-1958).....*Japanese painter.*

ACKNOWLEDGEMENTS

So many people to thank.

To my beta readers, I owe you much: June Almond; Leslie Beauchemin; Arlene Fliegler; Natalie Kerr; Cate Prest and Juleen Ruttan. And to Carol Branch, who kindly explained the ins and outs of pixels.

Thank You to Katy Phillips and Renato Rodriguez at the San Diego History Center for researching and answering my numerous questions. To Tomas Herrera-Mishler, President and CEO of Balboa Park Conservancy who graciously met with me and provided valuable information.

Thanks to James D. Newland, La Mesa, California Historical Society who dug through paperwork to furnish me with information about the "Flying A Film Company." And many thanks to Tom Frew, Jim Foster, and others at the Fallbrook, California Historical Society for their help and who caught my errors in Chapter 20.

And last, but not least, thank you to the Fred Harvey/Mary Colter Fan Club on Facebook where I found many useful photos and comments.

Note: I fudged some events to help my storyline. I take full responsibility for the fudging and any errors found in the final publication of this novel. The buck stops at my desk.

ABOUT THE AUTHOR

P. Austin Heaton lives in Southern California. Her passion is writing novels based on history. She can be reached through her author page on Amazon.com. Contact and comments are encouraged.

If you enjoyed "Murder at the Expo," please leave a review on Amazon, Goodreads, etc. Feedback is most appreciated and encourages others to the read the book.

Her debut novel set in 1861 America, *Deserter, Rebel, Renegade: A Fugitive's Search for Freedom* is available on Amazon.com.

Happy Reading!!!

Deserter, Rebel, Renegade: A Fugitive's Search for Freedom
– a historical adventure drama set in 1861. You are invited to read
Confederate deserter, Temple Hamilton's private journals filled
with adventure and a forbidden love. They document why he
deserted and his amazing journey across North America in the
early 1860s from the battlefield of Manassas, Virginia to San
Francisco, California.

Temple Hamilton was on a quest to escape his past. But even
3,000 miles away in San Francisco and the small gold mining
community of Angels Camp, it was going to be a difficult task,
perhaps impossible.

You, the reader, can cozy up with a cup of hot chocolate and
roll along with a wagon train carrying pioneering settlers and gold
seekers, meet some scoundrels and the woman he falls for but
can't have, receive a chilling fortune teller's prediction, befriend a
Zen Monk, assist a pompous Italian tenor, help a group of circus
performers, engage in mind-games with a Chinatown madam, lurk
in a dirty alley as a secret murder unfolds, etc. Enjoy a lively
adventure set in a time that no longer exists.